HUMCA

Dancing
on the
Moon

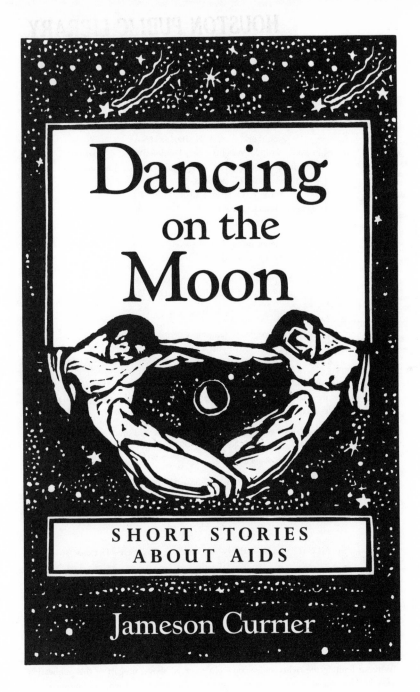

Dancing
on the
Moon

SHORT STORIES
ABOUT AIDS

Jameson Currier

VIKING

HOUSTON PUBLIC LIBRARY

VIKING
Published by the Penguin Group
Penguin Books USA Inc., 375 Hudson Street,
New York, New York 10014, U.S.A.
Penguin Books Ltd, 27 Wrights Lane, London W8 5TZ, England
Penguin Books Australia Ltd, Ringwood, Victoria, Australia
Penguin Books Canada Ltd, 10 Alcorn Avenue,
Toronto, Ontario, Canada M4V 3B2
Penguin Books (N.Z.) Ltd, 182–190 Wairau Road,
Auckland 10, New Zealand

Penguin Books Ltd, Registered Offices:
Harmondsworth, Middlesex, England

First published in 1993 by Viking Penguin,
a division of Penguin Books USA Inc.

1 3 5 7 9 10 8 6 4 2

PUBLISHER'S NOTE

These are works of fiction. Names, characters, places, and incidents either are the product of the author's imagination or are used fictitiously, and any resemblance to actual persons, living or dead, events, or locales is entirely coincidental.

"Civil Disobedience" and "What You Talk About" first appeared in *Christopher Street*; "Reunions" in *Certain Voices*, edited by Darryl Pilcher, Alyson Publications, Inc.; and "Who the Boys Are" in *The Right Brain Review*.

LIBRARY OF CONGRESS CATALOGING-IN-PUBLICATION DATA
Currier, Jameson.
Dancing on the moon : short stories about AIDS / by Jameson Currier.
p.   cm.
ISBN 0-670-84656-2
1. AIDS (Disease)—Patients—Fiction.   2. Gay men—Fiction.
I. Title.
PS3553.U668D36   1993
813'.54—dc20   92-50392

Printed in the United States of America
Set in Perpetua
Designed by Kathryn Parise

TO MY FRIENDS,
LIVING AND REMEMBERED

CONTENTS

CONTENTS

AUTHOR'S NOTE

These stories deal with the impact of AIDS. They are not intended to be a comprehensive examination of the epidemic.

Some of these stories were previously published, and I am grateful to the editors and publishers of those publications for their assistance and attention.

I would also like to express special thanks to my editor at Viking, Ed Iwanicki, for his encouragement and suggestions in the writing and compiling of these stories.

And I would like to thank Jon Marans, for his continued support and friendship, and Kevin Patterson, for the imprint he has made on my writing. Special thanks also to Anne H. Wood, Elizabeth Weinstein, Brian Keesling, Deborah Collins, John Maresca, Martin

Gould, Dr. Larry Dumont, Dr. Joel Byrd, Kevin McAnarney, Josh Ellis, Chris Boneau, Adrian Bryan-Brown, Jackie Green, Brian Hargrove, Jonathan Miller, Lori Epstein, Raymond Yucis, David Kagen, Karen Johnson, Darryl Pilcher, Jo Schneiderman, and David B. Feinberg.

Death ends a life,
but it does not end a relationship,
which struggles on in the survivor's mind
toward some resolution which it
may never find.

—Robert Anderson

Dancing
on the
Moon

WHAT THEY
CARRIED

JOHN HAD CARRIED THE FLOWERS SINCE PERRY STREET, LONG-stemmed irises wrapped together by a pale-pink tissue. Now he held them across his lap in the taxi; a patch of his khaki pants had turned dark brown from the beads of water which rolled down the stems. Danny thought John would have tired of flowers; once a week he had carried irises to Adam. This afternoon, on their way to Seventh Avenue, John had hesitated in front of the florist, and Danny, recognizing the confused look which had rushed across John's face, had instinctively scooped up the flowers from the white plastic bucket. Shifting the weight of the canvas gym bag he was carrying to his left shoulder, Danny went inside and paid a small Oriental woman, watching her eyes disappear into fine lines as she smiled and wrapped the irises together. Outside again, on the sidewalk, John raised his arms toward Danny, taking the flowers as though offering to hold a child. In the taxi, Danny lifted

John's hand and smelled his wrist, wondering why the fragrance of flowers never lasted as long as cologne.

o

Adam had carried only his briefcase to the emergency room. Inside was his wallet, his address book, a bottle of aspirin, and the reviews of the play he had been publicizing. Adam had tried calling John first, but he was out of the office, so he called Danny, because he was worried and wanted help quickly. When Danny got to the hospital, Adam was already in a private room and had a temperature of 103. Danny took the keys to Adam's apartment and brought back to the hospital Adam's pajamas, bathrobe, slippers, razor, shaving cream, toothbrush, toothpaste, and pillow. By the time Danny returned, Adam was asleep and John was sitting in the chair beside the bed, watching the sun set through the windows that overlooked East 79th Street.

The next day the doctors began their tests. Nurses drew blood and took away urine samples, though nothing was done specifically about the pain in Adam's lower back, which was the reason he had gone to the emergency room in the first place, Adam told Danny. John had to ask the nurses several times about getting some sort of medication to relieve Adam's discomfort, and finally got a doctor to order a prescription for Percodan. While Adam was being examined by yet another doctor, John and Danny sat in the waiting room, and John mentioned it wasn't the pain that had driven Adam to the hospital. He had been working too hard, had been trying to cover for his boss, who was on vacation. The producers were worried because the play wasn't a hit. Stress and exhaustion, John said, were the reasons Adam was here. Danny slumped down in his chair and rested his elbows against his knees, cupping his chin in the palms of his hands. Danny could tell Adam was thinner since last week; the youthful complexion had disappeared from his face, leaving behind an impression of bones and angles. Danny shifted his head till his eyes rested at a point somewhere beyond John. I wish I could believe that was the reason, Danny said. But I know it's not. Don't forget, I've been here before.

The following day John took off work and brought Adam flowers. Adam had not showered or shaved in three days. Lying in bed, he held the flowers across his chest and then asked John to help rearrange the pillows behind his neck. That night, Danny came by after work and brought the fruit salad that Adam had called and said he wanted, because, he added, he could not even stand to smell the hospital food. Danny had stopped at the Korean grocery on Lexington Avenue and bought a container of sliced peaches, melons, and strawberries, as out-of-season as the flowers John had found. John brought a bottle of orange soda Adam had called and asked for. While Adam ate, slowly and uncomfortably, John and Danny sat near the bed and watched *Hollywood Squares* on the wall-mounted television set. Before they left, Adam threw up the food, and John helped Adam change into a clean T-shirt, while Danny wiped the floor and rinsed the soiled pajamas. In the hall outside Adam's room, John mentioned he was surprised Adam was getting worse. Don't people go into the hospital to get better? he asked. Adam had been in the hospital only last month, overnight, for a blood transfusion. Danny said nothing but shifted his feet so he could lean against the wall for support. Danny knew Adam had already passed the point; the virus had become a disease.

Adam told John he didn't want any visitors. Only John and Danny were allowed to come by. I don't want anyone to see me like this, Adam said. They would be upset and hurt. Some would be angry, he explained to Danny. He would be better in a few days and then would go home. And Adam said no one could bring

3

him anything personal other than clothing and toiletries, not even a book or a radio or a *TV Guide,* anything, he noted, which would suggest he might be in the hospital for a while. After all, he said, I'm not planning on staying here long, and then, lifting his eyes to the ceiling and assessing himself realistically, added, I just don't want it to feel like a long time. In four days, Adam had dropped five pounds. He hated the hospital. He thought the nurses were inept; they couldn't even tell the difference between aspirin and Valium. They won't help me, he said. They can't stop the pain in my back.

And the doctors continued their tests: X rays of his chest, abdomen, and skull. There were bone scans, T scans, CAT scans, spinal taps, and another blood transfusion. By the end of the week, when friends found out Adam had not been at work or at home, the phone beside his hospital bed began ringing, and Danny knew the visitors could not be stopped.

Wes brought a new pair of pajamas after John mentioned Adam had already thrown out three pairs and several hospital gowns. Cheryl, Adam's assistant, brought a bag of Pepperidge Farm Gold-fish crackers, which at the moment she spoke with Adam on the phone was what Adam wanted, though they remained unopened in the top drawer of the hospital dresser. Roy brought current copies of *Spy* and *New York* magazines; Elliot brought Archie and Superman comic books. They all tried to smile, joke, catch Adam up on what was happening at work or in the news. They would clear their throats, change the subject, or avert their eyes when necessary, carrying their feelings inside, the way they knew they must, the way they knew Adam wanted. In the evenings, John and Danny would bring whatever food Adam wanted: lemon yo-gurt, canned peaches, pretzels, or taco chips. Most nights Danny stayed later than visiting hours, in case Adam threw up and needed to be changed.

And the tests continued. Steve brought an advance copy of the book he was editing on the Bloomsbury authors. Elliot brought scissors, which Adam used to clip his nails. Bob brought lip balm, which Adam wanted because he thought the hospital air was so dry. When the new pajamas found their way into the trash, John went to a discount store and bought six irregular large T-shirts, though Adam's favorite was the old gray shirt Danny pulled from his gym bag one night; Adam refused to wear it, instead keeping it rolled up next to his assortment of pillows. The office sent an arrangement of red and white columbines. Millie sent a basket of painted daisies. Roy brought yellow tulips. One night during the second week, Adam asked John to bring the bottle of cologne he kept underneath the towels in the closet of the apartment. If I'm not washing, he said, at least I can smell better than the flowers. When a postcard arrived at the hospital from London, from Harris, Adam spent an hour trying to calculate how long it had taken to arrive by overseas mail, how long he had been in the hospital, and what day Harris had heard he was sick.

Cheryl said to Danny she had never realized the small red bumps on Adam's cheeks were Kaposi's sarcoma; she had thought it was acne that wouldn't go away. After all, she commented softly while Adam was sleeping, he'll bring almost anything back to his desk to eat. Although I do, too, she moaned, but he never had to worry about his weight. Later that week, Adam told John food had lost its taste. It only has a meaning now, he said, and the next day he stopped eating altogether. The nurses began feeding him with a machine suspended on a pole which pumped solutions of fats and minerals and vitamins through plastic tubes connected to a vein in his right arm. Adam seldom moved from the bed now. When he couldn't manage to push the pump to the bathroom, the nurses brought urinals and bedpans but were still sluggish about bringing him medication. John began to have problems coping with Adam's illness. So Danny began to wash Adam at night with warm, wet cloths and brought cups and pans of water from the sink so he could brush his teeth. Adam said he still had the pain in his lower back and the doctors could not find the cause. It's not even a brain tumor, Adam remarked during a commercial between rounds of *Jeopardy*. He turned his head away from the TV set and began to cry. All I want to do is go out and see a movie, he said. At a theatre. With real popcorn and butter. The next day Adam had a biopsy of the lymph glands of his neck. Two days later a doctor brought the news he had Burkitt's lymphoma. Danny made Adam call his mother in New Jersey and tell her he was sick. She's the only family you have, and you have to tell her, Danny said. It's not right to keep it a secret any longer. On Saturday, his mother came to the hospital, stayed two hours, and cried. On Monday, Adam began chemotherapy. Adam told Danny he was honestly going to get better. Because now he was ready to go back home.

Danny was surprised three weeks had passed. Many days he could not find an order or sense of strategy to what had to be done, so he began to make lists: what to carry to the hospital, what he had to buy, whom he had to call, what he had to do when he got home. Danny carried the lists in his gym bag, pressed between the pages of his calendar. Inside, along with a bottle of ibuprofen, Danny carried antihistamine pills, decongestant tablets, and a box of cherry-flavored cough drops, because he never knew if the headaches he got in the late afternoons might actually be the start of the flu or a cold. There was also a comb, two ballpoint pens, a small scratch pad that Danny used to jot down notes, and a combination lock for his gym locker, though Danny had not made it to the gym since Adam first entered the hospital. Some days Danny worried the canvas bag would rip; when he added a book to read on the subway, and an umbrella or gloves because the weather could slip without warning between fall and winter, the weight would almost reach ten pounds.

The day Adam came home, John and Danny carried everything in duffel bags from the hospital to the fourth-floor apartment. Adam had been released and set up on a home-care program. A nurse would visit if needed; every night he would continue the intravenous fluids. Two delivery men from the home-care service carried up the stairs an infusion pump similar to the one that had stood next to the hospital bed, and three large boxes of supplies. Inside were vitamin, lipid, and insulin bottles, and an assortment of needles, syringes, and plastic tubing. Enough supplies for a month, a hospital representative told Danny. Danny cleaned the refrigerator to make room for the plastic bags of nutritional solution which Adam had to have for twelve hours each night. In his gym bag Danny now carried a change of clothing, in case he slept overnight at Adam's apartment; in his calendar he wrote every possible emergency number he might have to use. John made five extra sets of keys to the apartment, one for Danny, one for himself, others for Roy, Wes, and Elliot, so they could come and go as quickly and easily as necessary. Elliot went to the grocery store to get the things Adam wanted to eat: frozen turkey tetrazzini and pizza, potato chips, mocha-nut ice cream, milk, and mint–chocolate-chip cookies. Roy went to the pharmacy to get the medicine the doctor had prescribed: Halcion for sleep, Xanax for anxiety, Nizoral for thrush, Zovirax for the herpes sores in Adam's mouth, and prednisone, Bactrim, allopurinol, and AZT. Adam complained about taking so many pills. His least favorite were the large yellow capsules, which he said were difficult to swallow. His voice sounds so strange now, Danny said to John when they were alone in the kitchen. It sounds as raspy as if he'd spent a lifetime smoking, and he's always coughing to clear away the phlegm.

That night, John and Danny helped Adam hook up the infusion pump, following the instructions a nurse had written for them. Before he left the hospital, Adam had had surgery to implant a catheter in his chest, because his arms had turned into long strands of bruises where the veins had collapsed from being punctured with too many needles. It took John and Danny over two hours to do what the nurse had demonstrated in less than twenty minutes. They injected insulin and liquid vitamins into the clear solution of a plastic bag, connected plastic tubing to the bag and a bottle of lipids, and then suspended them from the poles of the infusion pump. They washed their hands and ran the tubing through the machine, then wiped the end with gauzes soaked in isopropyl and povidone-iodine. John panicked at every step, convinced Adam would be murdered by an air bubble. Danny continued, steadying his hands by placing his arms on Adam's stomach till he had connected the liquid-filled tubing to the tubing that hung from Adam's chest. Adam, too, was anxious and nervous. I don't want to go back, he said, and could not fall asleep. He refused to take the Halcion or Xanax and stayed awake, sweating and worrying and rolling the pump to the bathroom because of his diarrhea.

The first week Adam spent at home, everyone carried the hope he was getting better. Roy picked up Adam's paychecks and did the best he could to sort through what bills could be sent to the insurance company. Cheryl carried more insurance forms to the apartment. John did more grocery shopping; there never seemed to be enough paper towels, tissues, or garbage bags. Bob came by and trimmed Adam's hair. Elliot did the laundry. Wes took afternoons off from work to take Adam to the doctor's office for chemotherapy treatments. Danny arranged a meal service to deliver lunches to Adam in the afternoon. In the evenings, friends brought him dinner. Steve brought Chinese, Millie brought Italian, Bob brought cream of broccoli soup and an omelet from the restaurant where he worked. Adam said there was more food than he would ever eat, even if he did have an appetite.

When Danny arrived in the evenings now, he hung a change of clothing in the bedroom closet. His overnight kit, which contained soap, shampoo, deodorant, shaving cream, and a razor, found a permanent place by the bathroom windowsill. Danny slept on the floor beside Adam's bed; he was afraid of sleeping in the bed with Adam, because he was certain he would become tangled in the plastic tubes. Adam has always been a restless sleeper, John said. Before he became sick, he would toss so violently he would twist the sheet around himself till he cut off his circulation. When Adam could no longer make it to the bathroom in the middle of the night, even with help, Danny bought a bedpan, and John found the large plastic Donald Duck glasses to use as urinals, the ones Adam had brought back from his trip to Disney World.

Adam said afternoons were always the worst. He would be alone in the apartment, watching TV, when the depression would hit. But if anyone called, he refused to answer the phone, afraid of having someone hear the way his voice sounded. There were moments when Danny actually thought Adam was getting better. At least his spirits seemed to rise. At least he was eating. Every evening Adam would describe for Danny what he had eaten, how many bites he had taken, and if it tasted good or bad. Adam had also started coughing in his sleep, so fitfully Danny thought he wasn't sleeping well; Danny was surprised, then, when he asked Adam one morning how he had slept and Adam answered, I'm sleeping better than ever.

Danny learned Adam's thoughts went through a cycle. One day it was, Am I going to die? Another, it would be, Do you think I'm going to die? Danny was never sure how to answer Adam's questions. Once, when Danny decided to be honest and Adam asked, How do I look?, Danny responded by saying, OK. Adam lifted himself out of bed and walked to the mirror that hung on the back of the bedroom door, bracing himself by holding on to the doorknob. Just OK? he questioned, and began brushing his thinning hair. Please, he added, I still have my vanity, and he walked to the window and threw the brush outside.

The second week he was home, Roy and Danny took Adam to see a movie. Danny helped Adam walk down the four flights of stairs, his arms wrapped around Adam's waist so he would not fall because Adam refused to use the cane John had bought. Roy borrowed a car and dropped them off in front of the theatre on 59th Street. Danny found it difficult to concentrate on the movie, even though Adam felt certain it would be nominated for a number of Academy Awards. Roy bought popcorn and sodas, though Adam ate nothing, coughing and squirming in his seat the entire two hours. Afterward, riding in the car back to the apartment, Adam said he wanted to get tickets to see *The Phantom of the Opera* and take a cruise to the Bahamas in the spring. When Roy and Danny were alone in Adam's kitchen, Roy said Adam was setting himself up for disappointments. Danny replied, It's the way Adam has always lived. He needs to look forward to something. Later, in the bedroom, Adam told Danny, Today was the first time I was actually afraid of dying.

Danny was concerned that Adam was telling him things he told no one else. When Roy or John or Wes or Elliot was out of the room, Adam would talk about how he had not had sex since July because of the pain in his back. Adam said he felt safe when Danny slept on the floor, though he knew it was selfish to ask so much of him, but John was too impatient, Roy flustered easily, and they never knew what to do if there was a problem. Once, Adam said to Danny, I'm so afraid you'll be so disgusted you'll walk away. Danny promised him he wouldn't leave, though Danny knew there were moments when he wished Adam would die quickly. Adam himself could be impatient: Danny was too slow bringing the medication or could not pick up the tissues fast enough from the floor. The glass of water was too cloudy or cold, the TV was not loud enough or too loud, or Danny had left his fingerprints on the lens after cleaning Adam's eyeglasses. Adam had now dropped six more pounds; at night, he would stretch out his arms and remark in a rather wry tone, I'm beginning to look worse than a Biafra baby.

On Wednesday, Wes invited friends over to watch *The Wizard of Oz* on TV. Roy decorated the living room with a rainbow of crepe paper. Cheryl made green cookies to eat when Dorothy reached the Emerald City. Danny carried Adam to the couch in the living room a few minutes before the movie was to start. John remarked it was odd it wasn't Sunday. Remember, Bob added, it was always telecast on Sunday nights. Elliot said when he was a kid his parents always made sure they stayed late at church that night just to torture him. Adam said the worst punishment his mother ever gave him was not letting him watch it one year. He cried so hard she finally relented, letting him out of his bedroom just as the Wicked Witch disappeared in a puff of smoke on top of the thatched roof. Steve said, Remember when we watched it all in black and white? Or when we had to go to someone's house to watch it in color, John added. Roy said his favorite was still *Peter Pan.* Remember when Mary Martin sang about Never-Never Land?

The next morning Adam said to Danny, We can't go on like this, and laughed weakly. How many men have said that to you in your lifetime? Still trying to shake the sleep from his body, Danny sat on the side of the bed and held Adam's hand. I should go back to the hospital, Adam said. This isn't fair to anyone.

The moment Adam said he felt better was the time he was the most helpless, strapped in a wheelchair whizzing through a hospital corridor. It was almost fun, he told Danny later, all dressed in white, letting people I didn't even know worry about only me for just a few minutes.

The doctors began more tests: EKGs, EEGs, X rays, specimens, and cultures. The reason he went back, Adam said, was because he needed stronger chemotherapy, and he wasn't able to function at home alone the day after the dosages. He got angry only once, when a nurse said he wasn't trying hard enough when he refused to take a pill right away. He yelled back at her that she wasn't his mother. In fact, he added, I don't even like you, and besides, I didn't even ask for your opinion. The next day the stitching that held the catheter tubing in place fell apart. The doctor said it was impossible to perform the surgery again to repair it. Adam was too weak; now he weighed a hundred pounds. And an X ray showed a small black spot on his right lung. Another doctor said Adam wouldn't be able to sustain the amount of chemotherapy he would need. By the end of the night, the nurses had set him up on a respiratory system; oxygen rushed through plastic tubing to his nose. The next morning, Danny arranged for twenty-four-hour nursing care so Adam could go home. Adam had decided it was time to die.

It's not like I'm giving up, he said to Danny and John and Roy. It's just that I'm going to die naturally. Without surgery or therapy or treatments which would only prolong my life by a couple of days.

This time, John and Danny carried Adam up the stairs in a wheelchair. Roy went and picked up more prescriptions: Duricef, Compazine, nystatin, propranolol, and dexamethasone. A nurse was always there to give Adam his medication and make sure he would eat. Danny told John he felt somewhat relieved. Now there is someone who knows what to do about the coughing, knows when he needs to drink liquids, knows what time he is supposed to take a pill, knows what to say and how to deal with the pain. Someone is there to help him be comfortable. John answered, It isn't like this is all new to us.

Danny told John, Adam always had a fascination with suicide. Didn't he remember Adam reading *Last Wish* by Betty Rollin? The first time he was in the hospital, Adam had asked if Danny could find someone who could get him Nembutal—his doctor had refused to give him a prescription. Adam mentioned suicide first to Danny because he knew it would upset John. Adam said that he wanted to live, but the quality of his life had deteriorated beyond depression. I've spent the last two months waiting, he said. Waiting for doctors and nurses and medicine and food and visits and friends. Roy cried when Danny told him Adam wanted to die swiftly and painlessly, but Danny knew that Adam would not kill himself, that Adam had carried himself with dignity for so long, he wouldn't want his life to end with disappointments. Roy told Adam he didn't want him to do it, but if that was his decision, then he would do his best to respect it. But no one would help Adam find the medication. Adam complained it had been easy in the book. When Adam asked Danny to just open the window and let him jump,

Danny said no, and Adam said he would do it himself. Danny laughed and tried turning it into a joke: How could someone who has not moved from bed in over a week make it to the window and jump from the fire escape? I thought you were going to help me die, Adam replied. I'm sorry I'm disappointing you, Danny answered. Now you know exactly how selfish I am. I'm sorry you're more valuable to me alive than dead.

Five days after coming home from the hospital, Adam died. In the afternoon he began to have respiratory problems. The nurse hooked him up to the oxygen tank which had been placed by his bed. By the time Danny arrived, around 7:00 P.M., Adam was semiconscious, lying on his back, gasping for breath, his arms twitching as if he were asking for help. Danny reached for Adam's hand, thinking he might calm him, but he was shocked that Adam's skin felt as cold and lifeless as vinyl, so Danny rubbed his hands along Adam's arms, hoping it would help the circulation. Thirty minutes later, when the gasping subsided, the nurse rolled Adam over to rest on his side. She turned to Danny and said in a brisk whisper, Have any arrangements been made? Does he want last rites? Danny paced the floor till the breathing stopped.

The only time Danny cried was the day in the hospital when an orderly came into the room and shaved the hair on Adam's chest before the surgery to implant the catheter. John cried after his first visit to the hospital. Roy said he had cried while waiting in line to buy underwear. Cheryl cried when Adam called and said she could have the posters that hung over his desk. Wes said he cried in the steam room at the gym, when he knew no one was looking. Bob and Millie cried while having drinks together at the bar of a Japanese restaurant in the Village after they had tried to get Adam to eat the dinner Millie had brought. Elliot cried during the opening credits when *Auntie Mame* came on TV one night; he and Adam had seen it together on a double bill at the Regency. Steve didn't cry, or so he said, though Danny noticed he had started walking with his fists clenched.

In the hospital a doctor remarked to John that someone might carry this virus in his body for years before it began to deteriorate the immune system. Some people might not be affected at all. Danny turned to the doctor and replied rather sarcastically, Do you think we're all fools? We all know about this disease. Don't you know? Danny added. Haven't you heard? It's the fear every gay man carries today.

○

The hardest thing, Danny said to John during the ride in the taxi, was carrying the ashes. Danny had picked them up yesterday from the funeral home. They had been placed inside a cardboard box, small and rectangular, and the man at the funeral home had placed the box in a plastic bag. When Danny took the bag, he was surprised it was so heavy for something that small, estimating the weight he held was almost ten pounds. As Danny walked back to the apartment, the weight grew heavier; he couldn't shake the thought of what he carried.

John took the flowers to the kitchen of Wes's apartment, un-wrapped them from the tissue, and arranged them in a tall glass vase. He carried them to the dining table and placed them at the center. Around him Roy, Millie, and Elliot took their seats. The extra leaf Wes had added to the table made the room seem smaller; the air was warm and perfumed by the ginger he had used in cooking. Bob dimmed the overhead light, Cheryl lit the candles with the matches she found in her purse, and Steve circled the table, pouring glasses of wine. Danny asked Wes if there was anything he could do to help: Give me something to do, Danny said. Bring these to the table, Wes answered, pointing at two steaming plates of food.

As Danny brought the plates from the kitchen he paused at the window, noticing the way the rain bent the branches of a tree toward the sidewalk. This afternoon Adam's mother had called him. She had found the portrait which had been painted of Adam eight years ago, the summer when Adam was twenty-four. She described the picture, the way the artist had overlapped a sequence of pale-blue and green strokes, like a camera out of focus, yet had remarkably managed to capture the dimples on the left side of his mouth when Adam tried to hold back a smile. Then she apologized for not mentioning at the funeral that, when she saw Adam the day before he died, he had said, I feel so ashamed that it has to end this way. They've made it so much easier for me, and I've only made it harder for them. You know he loved you very much, she said to Danny. He wanted you to have the portrait. I'll send it to you soon, she added, and then said goodbye.

Danny had done everything he knew how to do; why, then, did he feel that wasn't enough? He straightened his shoulders to release the strain from his back and then carried the plates to the table.

CIVIL DISOBEDIENCE

I WAS FIFTEEN THAT SUMMER, THE SUMMER EVERY TIME YOU walked outside it was so hot and muggy it seemed the air was boiling. July was particularly oppressive that year; even the gulf breezes felt like you were brushing up too close to fire. I hung around Kip a lot that summer. We were both marking time; in August he was headed north to be an intern at a Memphis law firm for a month, and I was going to stay at a music conservatory just outside of Nashville till school started up again in the fall. Kip was already sixteen and had his driver's license, and his mother's car was air-conditioned, so we spent a lot of time cruising the street or hanging out at the mall. But most days Kip would get some sort of bug in his craw, he was always real intense, and he would huff and puff till he found some way to feel that his problem had been resolved, clarified, or vindicated. One day, a real scorcher, it was just after noon, and we had been lifting weights in the basement of Kip's house when Kip got into one of his fits and we jumped in the car and drove out to the mall.

"What kind?" I whispered to Kip when we were in the store, waiting for the pharmacist to turn his back to us.

"Any," Kip answered.

I reached up to a row of red-packaged condoms and plucked a box off the bracket, first holding it in my fist and then shoving it into the back pocket of my jeans.

"Let's go," Kip said and pushed me toward the doorway back into the mall.

"You want to put that back?" a voice sounded, and a hand clamped on my shoulder.

I looked up and saw a cop, the mall cop, standing beside us.

I let out a silly, high-pitched laugh. "I don't have anythin'," I said.

"You put it back and I'll let you walk out of here without any problem," the cop said. "Or walk up to the counter and pay for it."

Kip, angry, turned on the cop. "For almost ten years the government has refused to recognize a medical crisis that has spiraled to epidemic proportions. Our action is a political statement to support the movement for the national educational necessity for teaching safe sex in all classrooms."

The cop, ignoring Kip, said to me, "Put 'em back, kid, or I'm gonna take you in the back and show you how they're used."

Kip's eyes widened.

"That's sexual harassment," Kip yelled at the cop. "We could get you dismissed for that, pig."

"Put them back," the cop said firmly. The cop was not much older than we were. Kip once told me he had heard that the cop, Howie, got the job at the mall after he dropped out of high school.

"Now," Howie said, louder.

I reached into my pocket and slid the package back onto the bracket, embarrassed by the scrutiny of Mrs. Nichols and Mrs. Lenahan, next to us, looking at laxatives.

"Ahhh," Kip sighed, disgusted. "To remain inactive on the AIDS crisis is to be an accomplice to death."

"Kip," the policeman said, "get out or I'm gonna call your mother."

"I'm not scared of her," Kip yelled. "I'm scared that we're bein' killed by government neglect."

"Kip," the policeman said, "don't make me bring other people into this."

"Then arrest me," he said, and forced his wrists in front of the policeman's face. "I want to go to jail. I want to make a statement."

"Get him out of here," the cop said to me.

"Come on," I said to Kip. "Let's go."

"You're always backin' down," Kip yelled at me as we left the store. "Just when we're so close. We wanted to get arrested!"

"You wanted to," I said. "I don't need a record."

"Why does it have to take a congressional hearin' to find out the whole medical profession is understaffed?" Kip said. "There's no goddamn leadership and the President couldn't care less."

We walked to the other end of the mall, or, rather, I walked and Kip stomped, and we sat on the wall in front of the courtyard fountain. Kip pulled a pack of cigarettes from the pocket of his T-shirt.

He flipped one out for each of us, then lit them with the lighter he kept on a chain around his neck.

"They won't even arrest us for smokin' in the mall," Kip said.

"It's against the law," I said, practicing a smoke ring. "But everyone does it."

We sat there silent, blowing smoke rings up into the skylight.

"Put it out," Kip said suddenly.

"Why?"

"My brother is lookin' at us."

I looked across the courtyard and noticed Ross, Kip's older brother, standing in front of the shoe store talking with a group of guys. Ross was two years older than Kip, home for the summer from the state university, and working for a landscaping firm outside of Pascagoula.

"Why?" I asked Kip again. "Because he looks like he's hangin' out with fuckin' war criminals?"

"I didn't tell Mom I was taking the car."

o

"I am not a pervert," Kip said, slamming the palm of his hand against the mall doors. As we walked outside we were hit by a sudden blast of heat, and I bowed my head, squinting against the onslaught of sunlight, and followed Kip across the shimmering black-tar parking lot.

"I can't just stan' around and do nothin'," Kip said with exasperation. "Silence means death."

Kip was not an easygoing guy; there were days when he was wired tighter than a bomb. Short and solid, he was as agile as a tennis player but as restless as a racehorse. He had spiky blond hair and a chipped front tooth he refused to have capped because he thought it gave him a dangerous look. And at times he could be dangerous. He was prone to towering rages which would culminate in swearing bouts; once he even threw his fist against a window and ended up having stitches up to his elbow.

"I hate this place," he said, opening the car door. "It's so fuckin' hot." He took the beach towel from the back seat of the car and draped it over the front seat so that his skin wouldn't burn when he sat on the hot vinyl.

"How can you stand wearin' those jeans, man?"

"Easy," I answered. "They make me *feel* cool."

"And you think I'm weird," Kip said.

Kip had his left ear double-pierced, wore thin leather straps around his right wrist, and khaki shorts, and his T-shirts were studded with slogans or phrases or pins that said "Equality," "Act Up," "Come Out, Come Out," or "Play Safe." The one he wore that day said simply, in pink letters, "Pride."

"I can't wait to get out of this place," Kip said. "One more fuckin' year and then I'm out of here. Next year I'm gonna be in P-town."

"Right, leave me here to rot."

"We can get a place together for the summer."

"My dad'll make me get a summer job next year," I said, pulling my arm away from the hot plastic armrest.

"Once I leave I'm never comin' back to this dump," Kip said. "You can stay with me. You can get a job in P-town."

Kip had talked all summer about leaving Mississippi. But that day was his first offer for me to leave with him, to join him. It struck me as an odd addendum to his usual grumbling, but I had known Kip for years, and I knew his offer was genuine.

"Do you have any gum?" Kip asked.

"Nope," I said, and opened the glove compartment and put on Kip's sunglasses.

We drove to the car wash, then to get ice cream; then Kip decided we needed to spend some more militant time, and we went to Kmart and bought poster board, markers, and wooden sticks, stopped at the school parking lot and made placards, and then drove out to the hospital, just on the edge of the county line.

We paced in front of the entrance to the emergency room, carrying our placards. Kip's read "Tell Me Why?" and mine said "We all have a right to live." Soon the heat began to make us both edgy and Kip started chanting, "Who's in charge?! Who's in charge?!," which soon escalated in volume when I joined in. It was easy for me to be caught up in Kip's fervor, we had been best friends since second grade, and I yelled and yelled and stomped along with him. I noticed the nurses at the window of an upper floor looking down at us, pointing, and at the same time felt my body breaking out into a river of sweat. Kip began screaming, heckling people as they walked in and out of the electronic doors. Soon a security guard and a nurse with stern expressions were approaching us. I recognized the nurse as my neighbor Mrs. Donnell and stopped yelling. Kip noticed I had stopped and stopped himself.

"Hey, Buddy," Mrs. Donnell said to me.

"Hey," I answered sheepishly back.

"Why don't you boys come in and try heppin' us with some of these sick folk instead of yellin' so much?" Mrs. Donnell said.

"We are helpin'," Kip answered, his face squinting and puffing up. "If we're disturbin', have us arrested."

"Naaah." Mrs. Donnell laughed. "Nobody's gonna arrest you. But you two ain't doin' no good hollerin' out here. We don't set the rules. We just try to hep people. You got a problem, you should complain to the gov'ment. Why don't you write a letter to the gov'nor?"

"Tell me why medical costs are so inflated!" Kip said. "Tell me why insurance companies get to pick and choose who and how much they want to cover! Tell me why we're all gonna die from government neglect!"

"Jesus, Kippy, does your mom know you're so angry?" the security guard asked.

"Charlie Ray Fowler died at this hospital," Kip answered. "Because the government refused to acknowledge AIDS is an epidemic."

"It's so tragic about Charlie Ray," Mrs. Donnell said, shaking and bowing her head slightly. "He was a real nice kid. We're all just so upset by it." She put her arm on Kip's shoulder and it had a miraculous calming effect. She looked him straight in the eye. "You boys go on out of here. Stay out of trouble. I say prayers for his mama every night."

I noticed Kip's shoulders slump, as if he had dropped a heavy load of trash. "They'll never understand," Kip said to me. He turned to Mrs. Donnell, edged his shoulders back, and faced her squarely again. "You'll never know," he said to her. "You'll spend your whole life ignorant." He ripped up his sign and threw it on the ground, turned around, and walked to his mother's car. Caught in another embarrassing situation, I looked at Mrs. Donnell, then at the guard, then turned around and silently followed Kip.

o

Kip was his own rebel. At school he had developed a reputation as a weirdo punk and he had come to be generally ignored. Too often in the past, when a teacher had asked a question in class and Kip had been called on for the answer, he would digress from whatever subject was at hand—math, English, history—to his political argument of the moment, something like why the whales should be saved because no one needs to wear lipstick or how the ozone layer was crumbling because the guy sitting next to him was wearing too much cologne. Over the years he had alienated almost everyone except for me. Why we remained friends, why he never turned on me, I was never really sure, but I think it had something to do with what Stacy Lash said to me about Kip when we were all in seventh grade. "He has the biggest crush on you," she said. "He'll do anything to get you to notice him." For a long time I thought that was such an odd statement; I always considered myself too studious and serious-looking for someone to have a crush on, but maybe that really was one of the reasons Kip kept jumping up and down in front of me all the time, punching me in the arm or rubbing his knuckles through my hair.

After the hospital, we drove around some more in the air-conditioned car, stopped at the bookstore, stopped to get cigarettes, stopped to get gas, stopped for sodas, stopped to look at the construction workers building the new strip shopping center off Highway 63. Then we went to Kip's house to sit in the air con-ditioning and watch TV. After a few minutes of *Bewitched,* Kip again turned restless.

"We have to do somethin'," he said, fidgeting with the leather straps around his wrists. "I got an idea. Come on."

We were again in the car. It was late afternoon and the heat now felt as boxy as a winter coat. Even riding in the air-conditioned car, I could smell the trees and the grass and the sidewalk baking outside. Kip drove the car downtown and parked across the street from the police station.

"What's up?" I asked as Kip jumped out of the car, but he didn't remain still long enough to answer. He crossed the street and sat down in the middle of the road, right smack in front of the entrance to the police station.

"What's goin' on?" I asked when I caught up with him.

He looked up at me. "A sit-in. A demonstration," he said. "Like in the sixties, you know. Civil disobedience."

"Come on, Kippy, this could be dangerous," I said. "It's not like there are a hundred of us. Nobody's gonna see you sittin' down there by yourself. They're just gonna come on in and drive on top of you. Why don't you just do a hunger strike?"

He gave me a disgusted look. "I have to make a statement."

I looked around. The sun had dropped down, a fiery orange ball hung in the sky over Kip's shoulder, and I knew a driver, turning into the driveway, might be blinded by the light and fail to see the seated figure of Kip in the middle of the road. I ran back over to the car, found my placard, and crossed the street again. I stood behind Kip, waving my placard back and forth, just to be noticed, so Kip wouldn't be ignored sitting beneath me.

We stayed there for about an hour; cars pulling into the police station either went in the exit ramp or weaved around us by jumping over the curb of the sidewalk. Every few minutes a cop would walk out of the station entrance and look at us, spit something into a walkie-talkie, and then leave.

Soon I noticed Kip's mother walking down the steps of the courthouse across the street, not far from where we had parked the car. She walked right past the car and over toward us. Kip, once he noticed her, refused to look at her again.

"Kippy, my phone's been jumpin' off the hook all day 'cause of you. What the hell is goin' on?" she said.

She was dressed in a gray lady's business suit, a pink scarf knotted around her neck, and she carried a stuffed leather briefcase. She had dyed her hair red since I had last seen her, and I noticed, as she stood hovering over Kip, that her eye makeup was beginning to melt.

"People are dyin' and nobody is doin' anythin'," Kip said.

"And you think sittin' in the middle of the road is gonna solve the problem," she answered. "What about world hunger? Why don't you go protest in front of McDonald's garbage cans?"

"Stop makin' fun of me."

"I'm not makin' fun of you," she said with an exasperated edge. "I've been talkin' to people all day long about that missin' girl over in Leakesville. I've been drug in and out of my office all day into this heat. Kippy, I am not makin' fun of you."

"What happens if the government decides to quarantine anyone with the virus; whose side would you be on then?"

"Kippy, I'm on your side," she said, wiping away the beads of moisture on her neck. "But nobody's gonna take you seriously sittin' in the middle of the road on the hottest day of the summer. They're just gonna think you're queer."

"I am, Mom. I am queer," Kip said. "This is important to me."

Her face took on a serious and solemn expression. She shifted her briefcase, trying to think of something to say. She looked at me, then up at the entrance to the police station.

"Mel! Mel!" she yelled to the cop who had come out of the door holding a walkie-talkie. "Will you come and arrest these two boys so I can go home and eat a decent meal?"

o

The arrest was just a formality, but it nonetheless appeased Kip. We were fingerprinted, charged with disrupting traffic, fined a dollar each, which Kip's mother paid, and released in five minutes. Kip told Mel, the arresting officer, that he was being arrested as a statement against the government's inertia. We never even got to sit behind bars.

On the drive back to Kip's house, Kip convinced his mother to let us order pizza for dinner. We sat in the living room, eating in front of the evening news on television. Kip's mother spread her reports on the coffee table and started to read. Kip's brother, Ross, walked in and went right into his bedroom and slammed the door. A few seconds later he opened his door and yelled, "Mom, I got to talk to you. Tell Kippy to get lost."

There might have been a fight, except Kip was once again restless and he offered to drive me home. Outside, the darkness of the night made the heat finally bearable, and the breeze which drifted up off the coast felt good.

Kip decided to take the long route back to my house, but when we passed the cemetery, he pulled the car over and stopped.

"What are we doin' here?" I asked as Kip jumped out of the car.

"Come on," he said. "I have to see where it is."

We hopped over the cemetery fence and walked along the path by the wall, a sliver of moonlight lighting our way. Kip stopped at a grave and read the inscription on a tombstone.

"*Ante oculos errant domus, urbsque et forma locorum,*" Kip read. "I wonder what it means," he said.

"Somethin' like 'Thoughts of my home and the city are still in my eyes,' " I said.

"How did you know that?"

"I remember my mom tellin' me when she came home from the funeral," I said. "She's real close with Charlie Ray's mom."

"We'll all be dead before we're thirty if they don't stop this," Kip said.

I could sense his anger rising. He walked to a hill away from the graves and sat on the grass. I followed and sat beside him.

"What did you hear about him?" I asked.

"He was real smart in high school. He went to Yale and then lived in Los Angeles. He was some kind of movie lawyer."

"My mom heard he had been sick for two years," I said.

We were silent for a long time, listening to the sound of the traffic and the crickets. I lay back on the grass and looked up at the blanket of clouds that now covered the moon. Kip suddenly began to cry, quietly, but punctuated with deep heavy breaths.

"Are you OK?" I asked.

Kip leaned back and turned his body toward me. "Tell me it won't happen to us," he said, and pressed his head against my shoulder. His statement and sudden action left me with a loss of words, and I instinctively pulled his body closer to mine. The rest happened so quickly, impulsively. We began kissing each other, clothes were discarded, Kip pressed a condom in my hand, and I slipped it on. Instantly he was on top of me, and the night took on an urgency and passion I had never expected or experienced before. Feeling myself inside Kip, I grew dizzy; the friction of our bodies together, skin against skin, unleashed a measureless combination of pleasure and sweat. When he pulled off of me, the chill of the night air against my damp body felt bristly and awesome. Later, Kip told me that had been his first time, too, but then, as we lay there momentarily apart, I noticed the flash of red lights just beyond the cemetery wall. Kip noticed them, too, and he jumped up and grabbed his clothes.

"Come on," he yelled.

I grabbed my jeans and we raced for a patch of the woods and dressed hurriedly in the blackness of the trees. We crept as close to the wall as we could without being seen or heard, and we both gasped simultaneously at the scene in front of us. Kip's mother and brother were standing by a police car, holding flashlights, illuminating an officer pulling a body from the ditch below a portion of the wall.

We both ran out of the cemetery, jumped into Kip's car, and drove around town the rest of the night. Later we learned the body was the missing girl from Leakesville and Ross had heard a story at the mall about a friend of a friend bragging about a rape the night before.

But before we learned that, before Kip dropped me off at my house sometime the next morning, we drove around town with the windows rolled down, the hot air blowing across our flushed faces, talking about Ross and Charlie Ray and sex and Kip's mom and the dead body by the side of the road. Every now and then Kip would stop the car and we would kiss and touch and hold each other and Kip would rattle off a list of all the places we could go together. Then he would start the car and off we would go again, deep into the night. But what amazed me the most that night that summer was the way we didn't care where we were going. And how easily all the right roads materialized before us out of the dark.

WINTER COATS

ALL HE WANTED WAS TO DANCE IN A BROADWAY MUSICAL. AND he had spent years taking lessons to train his body to do so: ballet, jazz, tap, voice, acting, and karate. When he was a child his mother made him costumes: a leprechaun, a cowboy, and once, even, a sequined jacket. By the time he was twenty-seven he had danced in four Broadway musicals—one, a revival, he had a featured solo in and toured with across the country. But it was off-off-Broadway that I first met Dennis; we were both appearing in a showcase of a new play. I was twenty-three and had just moved to New York City after graduating from college, trying to find myself a foothold in the theatre. Dennis was twenty-two and had finished appearing in his second Broadway musical. But what was notable about this production, besides introducing us, was that neither of us was required to sing or dance. We began as fully clothed characters who talked nonstop in foreign accents; by the end of the second act we were silent and had completely disrobed. Now, fourteen years later, pausing in front of a shelf of thick wool sweaters in a store that describes itself as the world's largest, I am baffled by the paradox of the present, that Dennis has asked me, after all these years, the man who had the chance to admire his nude body close-up for a two-week run, to help him pick out a coat to protect him against the winter weather.

I have always thought Dennis was handsome, even now, though he is thinner than when he danced on Broadway. Until last spring he weighed 177 pounds, having built up his lissome frame in his early thirties by going to a gym. Now he lies and says he weighs 150. He is taller than me by two inches, five feet eleven, and he has light-olive skin and curly black hair, which he says his ancestors developed centuries ago in Greece. Yet, no matter how much or how little he has weighed, for as long as I have known him he has had a dancer's grace and poise; as he unfolds a blue cable sweater a salesman has handed him and holds it up in front of his chest, I notice his feet are placed perfectly in third position.

I started dancing late in life, though I had developed good coordination from sports—tennis, swimming, basketball, and baseball—abstaining from any sort of dance training because of the stigma attached to it in my small Missouri hometown. It was Dennis who took me to my first dance class, a month after that off-off-Broadway play closed. I remember, as I climbed the stairs to a third-floor studio and changed into a dance belt, tights, and T-shirt, how self-conscious I felt about it all, as though someone would approach me at any moment and say with a laugh, "What do you think *you're* doing here?"

There were about twenty other men and women in this class, beginner's jazz, which Dennis had assured me was the easiest one in which to learn the basic movements. I was relieved when I noticed that most of these other students looked like they had just walked out from behind a desk—secretaries, brokers, receptionists, and accountants—though I could tell by their determined expressions, the steady concentration behind their eyes, that they dreamed of being actors or dancers. The teacher, a man wearing a scoop nylon shirt and a bandanna around his forehead, was a friend of Dennis', and together they led the group through a series of stretches and simple movements of body parts I would never have done alone, at home, in front of a mirror. But there, dwarfed in a cavernous room of arched windows overlooking the grimy buildings of Times Square, standing between these other nondancers, I didn't find the movements so awkward or suggestive. After all, I thought, I am merely an actor trying to master another facet of his craft. Toward the end of the hour we did leaps diagonally, one at a time, across the room, then advanced to what was described as a pirouette, but what I discovered instead was a dizzy twirl, and finally a combination exercise of steps and lunges which we all tried to perform. I went back to the class several times, because I decided the conditioning was good, toning unused muscles of my body. Dennis was always there, and though I was never certain, I suspected that he and the teacher saw each other out of the classroom as well.

Dennis' strength was ballet, though he decided early on he would concentrate on jazz and tap, the road which at that time led to Broadway. Though his technique and training greatly surpassed mine, he would often stay after class and show me other steps. He would begin my tuition with the rigidity of an elderly ballet master, although, when I feigned awkwardness, my way of garnering more attention from him, he would become extraordinarily transformed into an eager boy showing a set of tricks to another. I watched him float through arabesques, glissades, brisés, and cabrioles while he showed me how to hold my arms, align my posture, and place my feet. Once, when I asked him to critique my series of jetés, he laughed and said, "You look as stiff as the marching brooms in *Fantasia.*"

Since the day I first met Dennis he possessed a set of characteristics I admired and tried for years to perfect: a beautiful body; a calm, sensitive disposition; a gracious, congenial personality; and a sense of humor which could leap spontaneously between slapstick and a clever, dry wit. Though he looked as a dancer should —long, graceful legs and lean, willowy arms connecting to a slender frame at sharp, tight joints—he was not narcissistic, as dancers often are. He was raised in Connecticut, by parents who, he said, made sure he was well mannered and educated, and who brought him into the city for lessons and shows, recognizing his talent and passion to dance at an early age. In fact, I envied him, not only on account of his good looks and commendable qualities, but because he always knew what he wanted and where he was headed. I have always been impatient, easily distracted, and try to avoid making any decisions at all. Often, I jump between an infatuation and a distaste for the theatre, racing to auditions only at the last possible moment.

Watching him now, as we ride the escalator up to the second floor of the department store, his hand placed against the rail as though he is about to begin a plié, I realize his decisions, his choices, his future were always directed by his body. On those days I watched him demonstrate a pirouette for me, he seemed exceedingly ethereal, as though unaware of the way women and men stared at him, some approaching with hope, wishing to charm and seduce him into their lives. Though he told me right off he had a preference for men, he detested the tiny, smoky bars of the

Village and the trendy, crowded discos renovated from unused theatres and warehouses, places which never failed to lure and enchant me. I went to these places in search of attention and camaraderie. Later, as I became more addicted to Manhattan night-life, I realized I used them as avenues for possible sex. Dennis had no such need for these places; as long as I have known him, he has never been at a loss for companions.

Dennis' first boyfriend I remember was the one who attended that off-off-Broadway play. His name was Brad or Chad or Tad or something like that, and I met him backstage in the small curtained space Dennis and I shared as a dressing room. I could tell Tad was the jealous type; he was extremely suspicious of me, and he stood with his fists clenched at his side next to Dennis, who was seated in front of a mirror, and began explaining why he didn't like the play, why he thought it was the wrong career move, why he felt Dennis should quit the production. Dennis' reactions were polite and controlled. Tad began working himself into a state near hysterics and I could feel him nervously glancing in my direction, willing me to leave before his anger erupted and he started a fight. The one time I looked at the two of them, Tad was holding Dennis' shirt with both hands, and I noticed Tad's face had become red and his eyes were wide and almost popping out of his skull. By the end of the run, Tad was gone, never to be seen again.

There were others, too: a television writer, a travel agent, a paramedic, a Brazilian financial analyst, a fashion designer's assistant, and several actors and dancers, though Dennis often told me he preferred not to get involved with someone in the same profession as himself. And there was a period when I didn't see or hear much from him. He was touring across the country in a revival of a Broadway musical, though I remember he once called from Oklahoma City and left a message on my answering machine. He said as quickly as he could that he hated the production, he hated traveling, and he hated the company, though he was having an affair with the stage manager, but anticipated it would end by the time they reached Houston. When I replayed the message, there was no number left so I could call him back.

It was almost a year later when I ran into Dennis by chance on Columbus Avenue and met his new lover, Joel, a tall, attractive man with a bewitching smile and a repartee of double-entendres that kept Dennis grinning. Joel was about five years older than Dennis, and neither an actor nor a dancer but a lawyer who worked for legal-aid cases for the city. Dennis began calling me again shortly after our accidental meeting; Joel did not share his fondness for movies and needed to spend most of his free time researching cases. Joel was a workaholic and clearly not as possessive of Dennis as his previous lovers had been, which left Dennis and me plenty of time to rekindle our friendship by going together to the cinemas around Times Square. I remember, the first few times I met Dennis at Joel's West End Avenue apartment, where Dennis had moved, how uncomfortable I was while Joel was around; my comments were stilted and simple, as though I were talking to a parent. Joel did his best to put me at ease with an amusing remark, whispering mischievous asides to me in a boyish manner when Dennis was distracted or out of sight. After I got to know Joel better, I realized he respected the time Dennis and I spent together. He trusted Dennis as much as he trusted himself, and, in a somewhat ironic parental fashion, entrusted me with bringing Dennis safely back.

When we reach the coat department on the second floor I ask Dennis, "Want me to pick one out for you?"

Dennis slips easily out of his jacket. "No," he answers matter-of-factly. "You have lousy taste."

o

Often the men I would meet and bring home from the bars or the gym were more stunning than the ones who latched on to Dennis. I have always been captivated by the beauty the male body could attain, perhaps the main reason I was first drawn to Dennis. That Dennis and I were never lovers, not even for a night, was not a mystery to either of us. Though I knew he was attracted to me, a fact I was intended to overhear when he announced it in a loud whisper to the director of that off-off-Broadway play, Dennis was the sort of guy who wanted a relationship with only one man at a time. I was more restless and adventurous. One night, backstage, I asked Dennis if he wanted to go out for a drink. "Only a drink," he answered. "Nothing else. I know your type. Who wants to wake up with a broken heart?" For years he would tease me about what he considered my major flaw: "Why is it that someone good-looking *and* smart still thinks with the wrong head?"

Sometimes Dennis would ask for details of my encounters with other men, beginning with the opening lines of our introductions. And usually I would classify my experiences for him, whether the sex was good, average, awful, or incredible. And there was always some moment with a man which stuck in my mind, like a song you hear on the radio and like but of which you can only remember a hook or a phrase. And when I described this for Dennis, the way one man's buttocks were tight but pliable like firmly blown balloons, or the way my fingers fit perfectly between the oblique muscles of another man's chest, he would become still and silent, his breathing short and heavy, as though enrapt in the viewing of a porno movie.

Since living with Joel, Dennis had never been unfaithful, nor,

I imagined, had the desire to be crossed his mind. Joel had started spending more time with Dennis as his career became more prosperous and secure. Together they took trips to Mexico, Brazil, and Europe, redecorated their apartment, and began to arrange dinner parties. Often, on the nights when I would talk with them in their kitchen as they prepared an elaborate menu, I marveled at how they now fully complemented one another: one concentrating on the meat, the other on the salad, yet both of them alternating chopping onions, shredding carrots, peeling potatoes, or embellishing each other's remarks with specific details. I couldn't help being envious of their relationship, begun, as Dennis once told me, the same casual way I had approached other men, a look while passing on the street, followed by another look and then an introductory remark. My tricks this way, however, were simply enjoyed and devoured, disappearing as fast as Chinese take-out.

When he turned thirty Dennis announced he was stopping dancing. "I can't dance forever," he said somberly to me one day on the phone, by which I knew he meant his dancing had become painful. He had started seeing a therapist, having been sidelined with pulled tendons and muscles. "And I did what I wanted to do," he added, and then asked me if I wanted to start acting classes again. We took a class together at a studio in the West Village, even though I had had some moderate success performing in a repertory company and a string of television commercials. A few weeks later, when Dennis started to worry that his body would become lumpish and paunchy if he abandoned all exercise, I convinced him to take a membership at my gym.

At the gym Dennis was something of a minor celebrity; several men had seen him dance, others simply admired his body. I was always awed by the sight of his body unclothed: tight and lean, his skin soft and luminescent as an unraveled bolt of silk. He seemed so youthful and innocent in the locker room of body-builders, and though he was constantly approached by men offering advice on how to broaden his shoulders, thicken his legs, and bulk up his chest, I think these men would have been happy just to take him home the way he was. Dennis easily became addicted to going to the gym; there he could stretch and work his muscles with confidence, without the fear they would be torn or damaged by performance. Sometimes he would go twice a day, first with Joel in the morning, then again in the evening with me. Once, when we stood side by side in front of the locker-room mirror in nothing but jock straps, I noticed that his pencil-shaped dancer's physique had been remodeled to the proportions of his athletic ancestors. I asked him how he thought I looked, and I knew, as he regarded my image in the mirror, he was trying to be both impartial and comic. "You have great triceps," he said. "Too bad mine don't look like that."

Now, standing in front of a mirror mounted to a column that rises to the ceiling of this floor of the department store, I watch Dennis, in a down-filled jacket, twist his waist first left, then right, studying the angles of the coat the way he once studied our bodies. He slips his hands into the pockets, hunches his shoulders, and pouts like a model, and then he bends his head down but lifts his eyes up, running his fingers through the strands of his thinning hair. Suddenly his face becomes pale and I notice his jaw clenching. He quickly removes the coat and hands it to me. "Bathroom," he says like a child with a limited vocabulary. I hastily rehang the coat and follow him up the escalator.

o

Years ago I had a friend who used to cruise the fifth-floor men's restroom of this store. Today it is empty except for Dennis and me. Dennis has thrown up twice and now stands in front of a sink, splashing water on his hands and face. When he finishes, I hand him some paper towels and help him dry his neck.

"OK?" he asks, as much a statement as a question, as though he had been waiting on me to leave. He grips my elbow with his left hand and leads me to the door, though I am not the one who needs to be supported.

Four months ago Dennis was hospitalized for pneumonia, brought on, he thinks, by the sudden chill of turning on an air conditioner to dispel the summer heat. He has known for ten months he has carried a virus within his body that is slowly, deliberately, destroying his immune system. For a while he neglected his diagnosis, or at least avoided thinking about it. Joel was also sick, having been diagnosed a year and a half before. Joel's first symptoms were swollen lymph glands, low fevers in the afternoons, heavy sweating at night, and constant exhaustion, attributed, he said, to his mounting work load. After Joel was hospitalized with pneumonia, he started Bactrim, had a bad reaction, and then switched to pentamidine, which caused him to develop scaly rashes and diabetes. Dennis stopped going to the gym, acting classes, or auditions and turned down a role in a daytime soap opera to stay home and take care of Joel. Joel, however, kept working as much as possible—half-days at the office, a few hours at home—but his anxiety over working, his anger over his illness, his terror of dying, and his fear of losing Dennis only made him grow worse.

Joel was not the first person I knew to become sick from this virus, nor the first I knew who had died. Though I had watched a friend lying helpless in a hospital bed slip from semiconsciousness into a coma, and Dennis knew a dancer who had leapt from the ninth-floor terrace of his apartment, our first acknowledgment to each other of our fear of this disease was at a Village café one night in a brief, apologetic conversation, questioning one another on the practice of safe sex. Yet, as other friends became sick, the shock of their deaths, the huge number of those infected, and the predictions for the future left us absurdly inarticulate with each other. The afternoon I met Dennis at a cinema on the East Side and noticed his posture was less than perfect, his steps were sluggish, and his speech was slurred, I knew, before even asking, that something was now happening either to himself or to Joel.

Once, Dennis told me Joel's illness was the most difficult and the most intimate period of their relationship. He felt strong being able to take care of Joel, helping negotiate the labyrinth of doctors, medications, and problems. He arranged a support system of friends for shopping, cleaning, cooking, and taking Joel to the doctor. He kept abreast of the latest treatments and therapies, medical and homeopathic, and together they experimented with meditation and visualization. At night, before going to sleep, Dennis would make Joel list the things that were bothering or depressing him, so Dennis would know how—could try—to make Joel's time more comfortable. Dennis was able, as if by instinct, to know when Joel was holding something back. Often he could finish Joel's thought before it was spoken. Over a period of almost two years, Joel battled pneumonia five times. A month after Joel's funeral, Dennis was in the hospital.

Now, thirty-eight pounds thinner, his hairline receding, his olive skin ashen, his eyes hollowed, darkened, by medication and grief, Dennis has entrusted his security to me and a new winter coat. He tries on a denim jacket, and though I think it looks good on him, he is able to read my thought that it will not offer much warmth.

"I just wanted to see what it looked like on," he says, his eyes widening as he looks at himself in the mirror.

Together we sort through the racks, and he tries on a wool

knee-length topcoat, gray and businesslike, and then a bright-red cotton ski jacket which has zippers on the sleeves. Even though Dennis knows I detest department stores—even the thought of shopping—over the years of our friendship I have helped him pick out a microwave oven, a video-cassette player, several swimsuits, and Christmas presents for Joel. Dennis likes to look at all the alternatives before making a purchase. Normally I have little tolerance for such methods; I usually know what I want before I ever enter a store. Once, several years ago, Dennis and I had our one and only fight, over some shirts I had rushed him into purchasing. When he got home and found they were long-sleeve instead of short, he called and demanded I pick them up immediately from his apartment and return them to the store.

Today I do not rush him. In fact, I point out other styles, other colors for him to try. Watching him change coats, I am again reminded of how our relationship has changed. In the last three months I have sublet my apartment in the East Village and moved in with Dennis, and together we have started him on a macrobiotic diet he had heard was successful. My last acting job, five weeks ago, was a day's work in a music video; I have told my agent the only work I can now accept must be short-term, and with the understanding I might have to cancel. When I'm not running errands, the remainder of my time is spent with Dennis. My greatest fear for now is that he will lose his will, his desire, to live.

Dennis slips on a goose-down-filled parka, dark-green cotton, with a detachable hood which dangles across the width of his back. An elderly woman, nearby with her husband, catches Dennis' reflection, smiles, and nods.

"It does look good," I say.

"Sold," he says, laughing, and turns to me. "Now it's your turn." He weaves through the aisle, stopping in front of a display of leather jackets so expensive they are chained to the rack. I shake my head, but before I can say "No," Dennis has lifted one up for my approval.

"Don't worry," he says, inspecting the price tag. "I know you can afford it."

o

When Joel died he left Dennis everything he had: his books, records, furniture, clothing, the West Side co-op, stocks, and a sizable life-insurance benefit. Joel's family had been well off; plans for his parents' retirement, medical benefits, and financial needs had been made many years ago. As Joel explained to Dennis before he died, his parents didn't need the money, and his sister and her two children were provided for by her husband. "Besides, I want Dennis to have everything," Joel said to me one night at the hospital. "After all," he added with a wry smile, "it's the least he should get for putting up with me for eight years."

As the beneficiary of Joel's will, and through Joel's system of setting up joint accounts and living trusts, Dennis has more money than he desires to spend. Though Joel did not know about Dennis' own illness until a month before he died, he suspected that Dennis, too, would become ill. He arranged complete medical insurance and a disability plan for Dennis, both of which now pay his bills and provide additional income. This morning Dennis asked me to hire a car and a driver to escort us around town; his request, I know, was intended to give our outing more ease, not propelled by whimsy or extravagance.

"I've been lucky," Dennis said as we rode downtown to go shopping. And I know he didn't mean his new, sudden wealth. He was feeling good; we had just left the doctor, who had told Dennis his T-cell count had stabilized and had written him a prescription to relieve the nausea. "I've loved and been loved,"

Dennis added with a wistful laugh, and stretched his legs out fully before him. "What more could I want except a little more health? There are people who have it worse off than me.

"Someone's going to be very rich when all this is over," he continued. "There's a pot of gold at the end of the storm." I offered no comment and turned my head away from him to look out at the street: signs, stores, and strollers whirled past my vision. He knew this was a subject I refused to discuss with him. Dennis has begun putting his money into joint accounts and living trusts, as Joel did before him, only this time the other name is mine. I told him I didn't want it, didn't need it; it should be given to charities or organizations that can use the funds and the help. Money can't buy for him, for me, what I want. It cannot buy time: past, present, or future. I can't purchase Dennis' health, Joel's life back, or something to erase my own fear of dying. "You don't have to use it if you don't want to," Dennis said when he told me of his plan. "But it's there if you want it." Security, as it were, like a winter coat.

Despite my objections, Dennis has purchased a leather jacket for me. Though he has enough money with him to pay in cash, he paid for both coats on his credit card. His reasoning is one Joel taught him shortly before he died: no one is responsible for a dead man's debts. Now the coats have been folded and placed into two large shopping bags, which I swerve either in front or in back of me to avoid hitting people as we travel across the main floor. Suddenly the store has become busy. Dennis walks ahead of me, sidestepping around the shoppers streaming in through the revolving door.

The car is waiting for us at the corner. Outside, I am momentarily confused by the bright October light, and, jostled by the crowd, I lose sight of Dennis. It is a crisp, clear autumn day, the air so light, so buoyant, not even the swarm of shoppers can agitate me. When I spot Dennis he is standing on the curb near the car. As I approach him he observes, just as I do, a street sign that reads "Broadway." And then there is a moment so private, so personal, it is priceless. Dennis smiles, making sure I notice, straightens his posture, and springs quickly from flexed knees to the balls of his feet. Effortlessly, gracefully, he spins through a double pirouette. I could never do even one without losing my balance. And then he is gone, dancing out of sight behind the opened door of the car.

REUNIONS

"I MAGINE," GLENN SAID. "THE IDEA OF IT."

We were seated at a window table that looked out onto Eighth Avenue. A bright crack of sunlight bent through the glass and landed on a row of bottles behind the tall, dark mahogany bar. It was late morning and the restaurant was empty. Glenn was on his second martini; I was still sipping my first beer. Though I have known Glenn for almost a decade, we hadn't seen each other in almost three months; our communication had been limited to phone conversations and notes left to one another on the refrigerator in our friend Peter's apartment. After Peter's funeral service, an hour earlier, we had walked the three blocks to this restaurant.

Glenn had just finished telling me the story of when Peter, in the hospital, decided he hated his nurse, a Turkish woman, so much that one day he started insulting her in French, which she didn't understand. The nurse thought, because Peter kept saying

"*Chienne, chienne,*" he meant he wanted the channel changed on the television set beside the bed. I looked down at the table, feeling momentarily guilty of my smile, then fingered my necktie, blue silk with tiny white dots.

I was surprised to see Glenn looking calm and rested. I felt both miserable and uneasy, having helped Peter's family with the details for the funeral. Glenn looked terrific, perhaps the best I had ever seen him: he had cut his light-brown hair short on the sides and in the back, his complexion was clear and healthy, red at the cheeks, and in his dark, tailored suit and striped tie he looked like a schoolboy who had just cut class.

"And you know about the last time he saw Kyle, don't you?" Glenn said, his brown eyes widening.

"I didn't know they saw each other," I answered. "I thought they just spoke on the phone."

"When they were both in the mood."

"When did he see him?"

"Just a couple of weeks ago."

"He probably forgot to tell me about it."

"He didn't forget about it. He was too busy being cranky. 'I need the tissues by the bed,' " he said, mimicking the way Peter would demand things. " 'You know this soup is too hot for me. But I don't *want* to watch *Casablanca* on TV.' "

I laughed again. In the last few months, when Peter wasn't in the hospital, Glenn had stayed at Peter's apartment during the mornings and afternoons, helping with the cleaning, cooking, shopping, and laundry; I had helped out at night, after work. Both of us had tried to keep Peter comfortable: he had dropped a lot of weight, the medications made him drowsy and incoherent at times, and he had lost a great deal of mobility because of the pains in his legs, the cause of which a squad of doctors and specialists couldn't discover or control. And every day we tried to keep him entertained, never an easy feat even when he was well. Many times we were both driven close to tears by Peter's bitterness over being sick, the constant stress of trying to relieve his anxieties, and our own helplessness and confusion, watching our friend grow weaker and weaker day by day. Suddenly I felt an odd tranquillity: a peculiar combination of sadness, reprieve, and lightness from drinking a beer on an empty stomach so early in the day.

"His nurse, the one that came to his apartment, told me it was because of the steroids," I said. "She said, if he was cranky before he started them, they would only make it worse."

A waiter approached the table, and we ordered another round of drinks. "Why is it that all the beauty in New York seems to be wasted on the waiters?" Glenn said as we watched our waiter, muscular and quite handsome with a dark mustache as wide as a comb, rock his hips as though dancing as he glided behind the bar.

"He wasn't just cranky before," Glenn said to me, though his attention was still focused on the waiter. "He was always particular. I mean, remember the time he canceled his subscription to the opera because they started to flash subtitles above the stage?"

The waiter returned to the table and placed the drinks on top of fresh napkins, scooping the empty glasses and bottle up with one hand. Glenn looked up and smiled. The waiter caught his eye and grinned, somewhat embarrassed, and asked, "Anything else?"

"Just a lot of wishes," Glenn said, lifting his martini glass in the air and shaking it lightly. The waiter made an uncomfortable bow and departed again toward the bar.

"Anyway, Kyle had been sick for a long time, almost two years," Glenn said, and replaced his drink on top of the napkin. "At that point he was worse off than Peter. He had just gotten out of the hospital a few days earlier. And he was just like Peter: the type that couldn't sit still. Well, it must have been like ten o'clock in the morning, and Peter was already in a bad mood, because he hadn't been able to keep any of his breakfast down. I was washing the dishes when Kyle called and said he was coming over. You should have seen the look of surprise on Peter's face. He made me stop what I was doing and find him a clean shirt and clean underwear, pick up the sheets from the floor, make the bed, and put new batteries in the electric razor. The whole time Peter kept mumbling, 'He's never going to make it here; he'll change his mind when he gets to the corner; he'll never make it up the stairs.' About an hour later the buzzer rings, and I tell Peter I'll go down and help Kyle up the stairs. Well, Peter started going wild and said that if Kyle had enough energy to walk around the block from his apartment, he could certainly make it up five flights of stairs without any help, and it would only make him mad if someone offered to help him. I mean, I could tell Peter was a little angry because he hadn't had the energy to go out of the apartment in almost a week. So we both sat on the sofa and waited. And waited. About thirty minutes later there was this soft knock on the door."

"How did Kyle look?"

"He was real thin," Glenn replied. "He had always been a little on the chubby side, but his arms had gotten so skinny he looked like one of those people I used to make with my dad's pipe cleaners when I was a kid. He looked worse than Peter ever did. He had lost most of his hair, but he had grown a beard. It made his face look so dark and glum.

"Anyway, he was standing in the doorway, wobbling back and forth, and the first words out of his mouth are, 'I think I'm going to faint.' But he makes it over to the chair near the television by himself, and he sits down. Peter wouldn't get up, because he didn't want Kyle to know he had to use a cane to walk. So they sat and talked a while: Kyle said his roommate had set up a computer for him on a rolling tray so he could play video games in bed, and Peter started remembering about the time they missed the bus coming back from Atlantic City because he couldn't pull Kyle away from the nickel slot machines. Then they both started complaining about their doctors and medicines. And then Kyle gets up and turns on the TV. Well, of course Kyle turned the channel to MTV, which I could tell made Peter livid, because, you know him, if it wasn't pre-1960 or British it wasn't worth watching. But they sat there and talked some more.

"They seemed fine, so I told them I was going out to run some errands," Glenn continued. "I had to get Peter's new prescription filled at the pharmacy, and I thought they might like some time alone. I must have been gone for about an hour, and when I got back, they were both gone. No note. Nothing. Well, I sort of panicked—I mean, these were not two young men in prime-time health. I even looked out the window, just to make sure they hadn't jumped. Nothing. I never thought they could have made it down the stairs and out of sight before I got back."

"How did Peter make it down the stairs?"

"He told me he had to help Kyle down."

"What?"

"They were sort of like balancing each other. And Peter didn't even take his cane. When one wobbled, the other one sort of wobbled the other way."

"I can't believe it."

"Anyway, I was kind of worried. I thought about calling someone, but who do I call? 'Hello, police, I'd like to report two missing homosexuals.' Then I thought maybe one of them had collapsed. If Kyle had needed help, Peter would have called an ambulance.

If it were Peter, he would probably still have been on the floor. I didn't think it possible both of them would need to go to the hospital. So I went across the hall and asked that Hispanic lady if she had seen them. If anything had happened, she would be the first to know. But she hadn't seen them. So I went back inside and called Kyle's number, thinking maybe they had gone there, but there wasn't any answer."

"What did you do?"

"I just waited. About two hours later the buzzer rang, and when I listened, it was Peter yelling for some money."

"Money?"

"It seems the two of them had gone for a cab ride, but neither of them had any money."

"Where did they go?"

"To the park. They drove around Central Park for two hours!"

"But Peter hated Central Park."

"Well, by the time I got downstairs with some money Peter was fuming. He had dropped Kyle off at his apartment. He had one of those cab drivers who don't speak English, and he kept telling the cab driver to go up the stairs and buzz the apartment so he could get paid. Anyway, Peter got so frustrated he opened the door of the cab and literally crawled up the steps to ring the buzzer. And the whole time this cab driver, who must have been just off the boat from South America, was flapping his arms and screaming, 'Pay me trip. Pay me trip.' "

"How much did the cab cost?"

"Too much! And Peter didn't want to tip the driver, because he was 'a first-class idiot.' I calmed the cab driver down, paid him, and helped Peter up the stairs. He complained the whole time. He said that after I left to go shopping, Kyle decided he was hungry, so he went into the kitchen and found the chocolate-chip ice cream in the freezer and sat down in front of the TV and ate the whole pint. And he was still hungry. So they decided to go down to the store on the corner to get some more. By the time they got to the bottom of the stairs, Kyle was huffing and puffing so much that they couldn't go anywhere, not even back up the stairs. So they flagged down a cab, but the driver wouldn't take them a half a block. So Kyle decided they should drive through Central Park."

Glenn pushed aside his empty glass. "On top of it all, the driver had no idea where anything in the city was. When Kyle said 'Central Park,' he must have thought he meant 'Centre Street,' because they started heading downtown. When Peter realized they were heading in the wrong direction, he started tapping the driver on the shoulder and saying 'No, No,' which got the driver real annoyed. He finally got the driver to turn around, but by the time they got to the park, Kyle had fallen asleep."

"What?"

"He kept falling asleep. They drove all through the park, and Peter kept nudging Kyle because he was sleeping with his head on Peter's shoulder and hurting his arm. Kyle would wake up for a minute and then pass out again. When Peter told the driver to take them back, he got lost again. They ended up on the West Side Highway. So, two hours later, the cab pulled up in front of Kyle's apartment, and Peter woke him up and helped him to the door and then told the driver to take him around the corner to his apartment. But you want to know what made Peter really furious?" Glenn asked.

"What?"

"That Kyle had eaten all of his ice cream. The reason he had agreed so hastily to go to the store with Kyle was because he was afraid Kyle would eat the butterscotch cake Suzanne made for him. Imagine, two dying *faygeleh*s riding through Central Park, one mad because the other had eaten all of his ice cream, the other so oblivious to everything he simply falls asleep, with a driver who doesn't even know what the hell he's doing. Two hours later I'm sure they all forgot they had even seen each other."

o

A week after Peter saw Kyle, Kyle died. Peter died less than a month later. Six months later I sat in a restaurant telling my friend Larry this story. We had both been drinking steadily for over an hour since we finished eating, and as we were leaving I waited with him at the corner to make sure he caught a cab. Watching him drive away, I was again baffled by the absurd uncertainty which had crept into my life. Glenn had gone quickly. Overnight. A cold had turned into pneumonia. Two days later he was dead. The last time I had seen him was the day of Peter's funeral, when he told me the story about the cab ride through Central Park. Walking uptown to my apartment, I remembered the way Peter would turn to me after we had walked out of a movie or a play or a restaurant and shove his hands deeply into his pants pockets and shrug his shoulders, knowing he was not yet ready to go home, and say, "Whatever should we do next?"

DANCING ON
THE MOON

MUSIC BLED THROUGH THE WALLS LIKE AN AMPLIFIED HEART-
beat. Eddie was outside, on the deck of the Pavilion, the palms of
his hands flat against the wood railing as he leaned into the warm
summer night. He rocked lightly back and forth on his heels, trying
to bridge the sounds of a syncopated drum to the constant whispering rhythm of the Atlantic waves. He stopped when he noticed
Bill was beside him, his figure eclipsing a portion of the full moon.

"I thought you wanted to stay," Eddie said, and felt a breeze
rise and slip between them.

"Not really," Bill answered, and ran his hand through his hair,
fingering the blond strands which the wind had blown across his
eyes.

Bill turned and Eddie followed, weaving through a group of
brightly dressed men. A flash of blue light blinked through the
door of the disco as Eddie passed by, making his white cotton

shirt glow as though he had slipped in front of an ultraviolet beam. In the darkness of the stairway, Eddie lost sight of Bill, and he hurried down the stairs two steps at a time. On the boardwalk, he quickened his pace, conscious of the way the planks of wood shifted beneath his feet and added a bounce to his steps. It gave him an odd feeling, he thought, part delight, part discontent, like a young boy dragging a balloon home before the circus had left town.

"Let's take the beach back," Eddie said when he had caught up with Bill.

Bill nodded and shoved his hands into the pockets of his jeans.

At the intersection of two lanes they drifted to the left, traveling between houses perched on stilts above the sand. The boardwalk dipped and climbed a dune. Eddie's heart jumped as the ocean came into view and the moon slid across the top of the water. Bill said nothing but bent his head toward Eddie, as though waiting for him to speak. Eddie remained silent but shifted his shoulders slightly, continuing his pace and staring straight ahead.

Eddie had thought about the beach all week; in August the city was muggy and oppressive. He could never reach work without becoming drenched in sweat, and the drone of the air conditioner in his office sent him home with headaches. Bill had hesitated about leaving the city, but Eddie explained there would be plenty of distractions: they could spend the afternoon on the beach or take a walk to the Grove, in the evening there was Tom and Allan's party, and afterward, if they didn't want to go dancing, they could always stay in and watch a movie. On the ferry across the bay Eddie carried a bag of books he had bought the night before, when he had wondered what they should do if it rained. Bill held another bag, which contained boxes of games: Monopoly, Scrabble, and Trivial Pursuit.

Eddie stumbled on a board and stopped, momentarily confused by the way the moonlight brightened some planks and left others gray or completely lost in shadows. Bill paused in front of him. The moon was straight ahead. It reminded Eddie of a volleyball, and all he had to do was play the game. Push the ball over the net. Bill would turn around and hit it back into the air.

That's what they had done at the beach today. They had played the games. Not just volleyball and Frisbee, but also the game of observation, a game that demanded little concentration, just a pair of roving eyes to watch the parade of men in front of the water. The ocean was as still as a pond, the surf only a few inches high, and beneath a cloudless, Crayola-blue sky the sand was covered with bodies, stripped and simmering under the sun. This was why they came here every summer, Eddie told himself when he lay on an oversized towel, the smells of suntan lotion, salt water, and sweat rippling together in the air above him. On the radio Eddie had heard that tomorrow the weather would be just as wonderful. He was glad. It seemed to infuse everyone with a tranquil energy, suspending for a while any pressure or trouble.

When the boardwalk ended, Eddie sat on the top step and unlaced his sneakers, noticing the way the moonlight magically made the dark hair on his arm seem blond. Bill stood on one leg and then on the other, leaning and pulling his shoes off with ease, then tying the laces together through a belt loop of his jeans so that the shoes dangled freely just below his hip.

On the beach the sand felt surprisingly chilly, and Eddie squeezed and curled his toes for warmth as he walked. Carrying a sneaker in the palm of each hand, he outspread his arms and waved them from side to side as though treading a tightrope. Finally, he felt released from the anxiety he had carried all day. This summer, with Mike's absence, Eddie felt the need to have plans. Mike had always made the summers seem spontaneous, collecting invitations to parties the way a child gathered seashells. Earlier this evening, Eddie and Bill had gone to Tom and Allan's party. Eddie knew it wouldn't be the type of party Bill used to work at as a bartender in the city. It wouldn't be like the legendary Fire Island parties either, the ones with suggestions to come in red, come in white, or maybe leather. There wouldn't be any bartenders or costumes at this party. Tom and Allan had just returned from Paris, and the party was planned as a simple dinner for friends.

Eddie had been concerned that the party might be uncomfortable for everyone. Tom and Allan had not been at the beach this afternoon. Before they left two weeks ago for Paris, Allan had noticed a small spot on his neck and a doctor had diagnosed it as Kaposi's sarcoma. It seemed an awkward time to give a party, though Eddie was grateful for the opportunity to be together. It gave them something to do, a place to be, a chance to lend each other support in a subtle, unspoken way. Tom and Allan had decorated their house with paper lanterns and jasmine-scented candles, and served pasta with artichokes, grilled swordfish, and a frozen cappuccino soufflé to twelve friends. Bill showed Tom how to make blue margaritas, and Allan passed around photos he had taken from the top of the Eiffel Tower. Eddie tried to stay in constant motion, circulating through the rooms with napkins, plates, and buckets of ice, aware that Bill was scrutinizing his every move. During dinner, Allan said Paris was as romantic as he had envisioned: the cafés, the museums, especially the boat ride along the Seine. Eddie decided the party must have been Tom's sug-gestion, just as the impromptu trip to Paris had been.

Afterward, while Eddie was helping Allan wash the dishes in the kitchen and Bill and Tom were cleaning the living room, a song came on a tape Tom had made three years ago. It was the

Supremes singing "Where Did Our Love Go?" Eddie became nervous and walked to the door that separated the rooms. Tom seemed frozen to the floor, unable to move, but when Bill started rocking his legs back and forth in time to the music, Tom relaxed and joined in. Watching them made Eddie achingly miss Mike. Mike would have stopped everything, walked to the center of the room, and matched his lips to Diana's voice, swinging his arms in all directions as if he had actually practiced the choreography. It was Mike who had said Allan would settle down. Eventually. We all went through that stage. But it was Eddie who had suffered through Allan's turbulent period. Allan got hooked on coke and started tricking with guys for money. Eddie often wondered if he had ever really had a relationship with Allan, or had it been just an affair that lasted too long? It was ironic, Eddie thought, that it was Allan who had kept the relationship going with Tom for over three years while Eddie had passed through a succession of beds.

Eddie stared at the moon, half expecting it to suddenly spin and twirl in the sky like a spotlight in a disco. He paused and asked Bill how he thought Tom and Allan had looked tonight. "All right," Bill said, easing onto the strip of hard, wet sand. Eddie made a series of large, brisk strides until he was once again beside Bill. Eddie thought Allan had looked great; the face that had intrigued a city of men seemed untouched. It was Tom who looked tired and troubled.

Even if Bill had detected a change, Eddie knew Bill would not acknowledge it. It was what he had done with Mike. Eddie had never seen Bill cry about Mike, though he knew Bill was not cold and indifferent. Some people reacted differently, even if it was a refusal to react at all. Eddie had always felt Bill held too much inside; now, at the slightest hint of sympathy, Bill would tense and walk away. Eddie believed Bill felt responsible for Mike's death. Bill had slept with other men. But so had Mike. Eddie remembered Bill at the hospital, struggling to lift Mike's spirits, hoping to squeeze a laugh out of him by doing something silly, like pinning flowers and fruit to a towel and wrapping it around his head, dancing about the room like Carmen Miranda, never once admitting the possibility of death. When Mike died, Bill was leaning against the edge of the hospital bed, drawing a clown's face on a white sock. Eddie had sat staring at an arrangement of daisies, trying to contain his horror.

Bill stopped and stretched, pressing his hands against his lower back and arching his chest toward the sky, a habit Eddie had noticed Bill had started, to release the stress. The sound of laughter floated from the direction of a house and Eddie turned and glimpsed two figures emerge through a door, their T-shirts and sneakers disappearing quickly into the night. The tragic mistake, Eddie decided, was that a stranger would still question their lives. Why were they still giving parties? Why were they still dancing? Wouldn't their fear make them reclusive? Eddie would answer that they wanted to be together. They *had* to be together. And though the wild, campy times had become wary and reserved, Eddie was thankful just to be alive and worried. Bill cut across the sand toward a path through the dunes. Before they reached the house, Eddie asked Bill if Tom had hinted whether Allan had started treatments. "No," Bill answered. "And I didn't want to ask."

o

Mike had been adamant about the beauty of certain things: the symmetry of a physique, the color of a cocktail, the way the summer sun, setting, polished the landscape with amber. Every summer, Mike had led them to tea dance at the bar in the harbor, where beauty assembled its pieces together into a late-afternoon puzzle. This afternoon, there were faces Eddie had never seen in the ten years he had been coming to the Pines, but that wasn't what pleased him. It was the ones that had returned. Eddie was relieved to recognize a familiar face. Eddie and Bill had lingered longer than they had anticipated, talking with Wayne, a friend of Eddie's from his first summer on Fire Island, who had traveled all the way from Minnesota just to spend the weekend.

"This is what I remember most," Wayne had said, and lifted his drink as though proclaiming a toast. "All the beautiful boys with reflections in their eyes."

"It must be tough to be young and pretty today," Eddie said.

"Look but don't touch," Wayne added.

"Touch but don't feel," Bill said.

"We were like that," Wayne said.

"Tough? Young? Or pretty?" Bill asked.

"All of the above," Wayne answered.

"Is it harder for them or harder for us?" Eddie questioned.

"Look at that one," Wayne said, tipping his chin toward a young man wearing a tank top.

Eddie turned and studied the dark, exotic youth. Years ago, Mike would have leaned close to Eddie and whispered some piece of gossip, something like, "He was the one last night in nothing but feathers," or, "I heard he spent the entire afternoon in the dunes." Those first summers, Eddie had been obsessed with sex. He had had sex on the beach, beside pools, and underneath the moon. Sex before parties, after dancing, between sheets sprinkled with fine grains of sand. Was what he had done, he thought now, more reckless than what two teenagers did on a dark suburban street in the back seat of a car?

Eddie glanced around the room of men, suddenly aware of how

time had passed. Should he feel guilty today about a virus that years ago he hadn't known to exist? Had his terror created an absurd game of guessing: who has it, who doesn't, which one of us is going to go next?

Wayne nudged Eddie in the side as the dark young man moved to another spot. "Do you realize," Wayne said when the youth had disappeared, "you've probably already had him? If you slept with one of us, you've slept with all of us."

○

Bill and Mike and Tom and Allan were Eddie's closest friends. At some point, for some time, if only just a night, each of them had been his lover. It was sex that had introduced them and kept them together. Eddie and Mike had been best friends since college. Together, they had owned a graphic-design company in Greenwich Village. Eddie and Tom had met at a gym in Chelsea, but it was Mike who had introduced Eddie to Allan in the lobby of the Met. Eddie, in turn, had introduced Allan to Tom. Eddie and Bill had met at a party where Bill was a bartender. Mike had met Bill when he went to a bar with Eddie. Bill and Mike had been lovers for seven years. Sometimes Bill said it was Eddie who had kept Bill and Mike together for so long. Eddie had not only solved every business crisis but had exposed the frustrations of one-night stands. It angered Eddie that Bill might think that way, as though Eddie's success in business and casualness with lovers had produced a life less fulfilling than Bill's. Or was it that Bill felt it should have been Eddie who was sick, that the wrong person had grabbed a seat in a bizarre round of musical chairs? Certainly Bill must realize that no one understood exactly what was happening. One unexpected death did not diminish the probability of another. Wayne had even mentioned this afternoon that there was still the likelihood that any of them could develop a regular disease, something like diabetes or meningitis.

"OK?" Bill asked. They were back at the house.

Eddie nodded. He was standing at the glass doors which led to a deck and the beach and the black waves lapping the shore. In the reflections of the glass Eddie thought his eyes looked puffy and dull, as though he had drunk too much or had taken too many drugs. Eddie felt the pressure of perspiration thickening the pores of his brow. This wasn't the way it was supposed to happen. In spite of their perplexing behavior, or, maybe, because of it, Eddie knew he and Bill had fallen in love. But it was impossible to remove Mike from the picture. Afraid of crying, Eddie walked toward the kitchen without saying a word.

Lately, when Eddie was depressed, Bill had been unable to provide the humor he had administered to Mike. All Bill could offer, Eddie knew, was his refusal to leave Eddie alone. Bill would follow Eddie, watching every move, waiting for the anguish to erupt. Sometimes Eddie felt Bill wanted him to cry—that his display of emotion would preclude any from Bill. Yet, if Eddie tried to touch or comfort Bill, Bill would back away, shake his head, or leave the room. The aftershock of Mike's death had produced a curious alliance between them. In the last two weeks, Bill had moved into Eddie's apartment in the city and Eddie had sold the business and started a new job uptown at an advertising firm. Now Eddie had learned to accept Bill's presence as if he were a shadow. But he was also aware that Bill was afraid of being alone.

Eddie drank a glass of water in front of the kitchen sink, and then, impulsively, slipped his head beneath the faucet of cold water. He shivered and grabbed a dish towel and dried his face and hair.

Walking into the hall, he imagined a breeze wandering through the house like a ghost, even before he discovered the glass doors were open.

Bill was outside, on the deck, in one of the canvas chairs, reclined as though he were trying to darken his tan. He had undressed to his underwear. His eyes were closed. Eddie thought about placing his hands on Bill's shoulders, gently massaging the sleep away. But Eddie was still uncertain Bill would allow even such a simple touch. It was odd, Eddie knew, how much they needed each other, how much they cared, deeply, for one another, yet, since Mike's funeral seven months ago, nothing physical between them had transpired. Eddie went inside and found a large red beach towel and went back outside and draped it over Bill. He sat on the top step that led to the beach and pulled his legs up against his chest, clasping his arms around them and rocking his body slowly back and forth.

This afternoon, on the beach, Eddie had been startled by a woman standing in front of him. She wore a floppy wide-brimmed hat and a baggy, pale-blue sundress, and as she spread her legs apart on the sand and crouched, the hem of her dress dangled beneath her ankles, blackening as it began to soak up water. She raised a camera to her face and leaned toward the ocean. Bill had been swimming and was approaching in her direction, his long, firm legs leaving behind a trail of salty white foam. Bill lifted his hands to his forehead and pushed the wet hair away from his eyes, unaware of the woman focusing on him. Eddie had wondered what the woman hoped to capture. Was it the way Bill's body, sturdy and defined as a gymnast's, glistened with water as though painted with oil? Or was it the way he moved, graceful and calm, nothing to indicate that the slightest movement could be too painful to perform?

The waves continued, rising and falling like sleeping breaths.

The evening air flapped through Eddie's shirt. Eddie doubted the weather tomorrow could be the same. Nothing is ever the same, he decided. Every wave moved closer or farther than the one before. He was thirty-six years old and had not had sex in over a year. Yet it was still hard for him to believe this was the summer of 1985 and four friends were already dead, another was in the hospital, and three more had been diagnosed. When would this nightmare end?

Eddie tilted his head toward the moon. Would a stranger confuse Bill's repose and Eddie's rocking for exhaustion and intemperance? The consequence and reparation of lives too extreme? Would a stranger understand their lives, or were they still full of misconceptions? Having been there, having seen them at the bars, the gyms, the baths, the discos, the beaches, would a stranger understand the unbearable sorrow which had punctured their souls so profoundly it was now granted the same recognition as the sound of waves crashing against the sand? Wayne had mentioned at tea dance that life in Minnesota still seemed mild compared with all this activity. "No one out there has a clue as to what our lives are like," he said to Eddie. "They think we haven't changed a bit. All this is as strange to them as dancing on the moon."

A young man strolling home alone on the beach as the sun is beginning to rise, the music from the Pavilion still pulsing in his blood, would notice Eddie and Bill on the deck. The young man would not wonder. He would know. These were not giant leaps but cautious steps, one foot carefully placed in front of the other.

MONTEBELLO VIEW

Jerry's hands were cold and chapped, and his arms, folded lightly across his chest, ached from his fingers to the joints of his shoulders. He wore his high-school basketball jacket, now too small for the width of his back, and the seams of the sleeves cut through his sweatshirt and pinched the skin underneath his arms. He slumped down farther into the seat of the van, the leather cracking as it rubbed against the vinyl cushion, and he shifted his hips so the weight of his body pressed more comfortably against the base of his spine.

"She won't remember any of it tomorrow," Ethan said, his eyes pinned straight ahead as he drove through the snow.

"Doesn't matter," Jerry replied, and looked out the side window. It was late afternoon and the snow, which had been falling since early morning, had transformed the bleakness of the highway into ribbons of black and white. Jerry watched a red Chevy move slowly in the lane beside him, the driver's face appearing and disappearing as the snow rose and flurried between the cars. Even now Jerry felt Ethan's mother, Mrs. Moeller, watching them from the window of her sixteenth-floor apartment in Virginia, jiggling her ice cubes in her glass the way two loose bolts were rattling across the empty metal floor of the van.

Last night the van had been loaded with Ethan's furniture: a sofa bed, a table, three chairs, and several stacks of boxes. This morning Jerry and Ethan had made at least twelve trips in the elevator, moving the furniture from the van to an empty room in Mrs. Moeller's apartment. They had finished before noon, and Ethan's mother, after spending the morning in front of a mirror applying layers of makeup, entered the crowded room and ran the tip of her finger across the dust of the table. "I never approved of the way you lived," she sighed, and jiggled the ice cubes in the glass she carried in her other hand. Jerry left the room before his anger could erupt, retreating to Ethan's bedroom to repack his overnight bag.

Jerry had not always resented Mrs. Moeller. When the phone calls began, he was at first sympathetic. Mrs. Moeller would call and tell Ethan she had slipped and twisted her ankle, and while trying to phone the doctor she had dropped and shattered a glass. Ethan, five hundred miles away, would stiffen his back and panic. He would try desperately to reach a doctor or an ambulance by long distance. Once, when she called at three o'clock in the morning, Jerry answered and Mrs. Moeller began to scream when she heard his voice. Though they had never met, Mrs. Moeller accused Jerry one night on the phone of taking her to India, where she had contracted dysentery. Before Jerry could wake Ethan and hand him the phone, Mrs. Moeller was crying because she thought she had broken her hip.

"She only does it because she wants attention," Jerry had said to Ethan the next morning. "She has nothing else to do, so she invents these bruises and diseases so you'll come running to her."

"The doctor said she's started to have blackouts," Ethan replied. That weekend he flew down to spend time with his mother.

Jerry had imagined several other ways it would end: another man, maybe a woman, perhaps a heart attack or pneumonia, or even by accident or an Act of God. Sometimes he expected, perhaps, a subconscious economic distinction might pull them apart. He never expected he would lose Ethan because of his mother's health. Since November, Ethan had flown every weekend from Boston to Washington. Now, two months later, a doctor had told Ethan his mother needed constant care.

Jerry expected more of a fight from Ethan; for years his mother had barely spoken to him, because she disapproved of his homosexuality, and now, wealthy from owning the apartment building she lived in, she could afford to hire a live-in nurse or move to a nursing home. Perhaps Ethan expected more of a fight from Jerry, a refusal to help move the furniture or a rage of hysterics at feeling suddenly abandoned. After all, Ethan had said his mother had been dying for years. She had always been arthritic or anemic and complained of migraines and fevers. When Ethan was a teenager, Mrs. Moeller had both a hysterectomy and a mastectomy in the same year. Now a doctor said she had suffered a series of minor strokes, and if she continued to drink and smoke, she risked the possibility of heart surgery. Last night, when they reached the outskirts of Washington, Jerry had wondered what would have kept Ethan from moving. If Jerry were sick, would Ethan have decided to stay?

The van smelled of cigarettes, though neither of them smoked, and a thin, dry taste pressed and scratched at the back of Jerry's mouth. He cleared his throat and the sound made Ethan avert his stare momentarily from the highway. Earlier today, Ethan had suggested, since Jerry was tired, maybe he should consider spending an extra day before returning to Boston. Jerry said he wanted to get back to the city; he had to be at work tomorrow, and the apartment needed cleaning and rearranging. Jerry told Ethan he could drop him off at a subway stop in Washington, on their way to the garage where they were to return the rented van. Jerry had decided, because of the snow, it would be easier for him to take the subway to the train station. Ethan could take a taxi back to his mother's apartment; Jerry would catch up on his sleep on the trip back to Cambridge.

Last night, Jerry had had trouble falling asleep. At first he thought it was a repercussion of driving so long in the tumbling van, the way his body had once felt numb and unsteady from riding a roller coaster too many times. Then he thought it might be the bed he shared with Ethan; the mattress was lumpy and much smaller than their own. Jerry got out of bed and wandered about Mrs. Moeller's darkened apartment. In the kitchen, while rinsing a cup he had used to make tea, he finally recognized what had been troubling him all day. Jerry and Ethan had been lovers for only eleven months. For years Jerry had lived alone. He had just gotten used to being with Ethan, depending on and being depended upon, planning and sharing, and now, he realized, he had already begun to distance himself from Ethan. It began when they loaded the van in Boston; Jerry's only words had been perfunctory remarks about what to carry and how to pack. The trip in the van had been mostly in silence, broken only by the confusion over which exit to take. Jerry was sure Ethan had sensed the withdrawal and had tried to bridge the chasm when he unlocked the door of his mother's apartment.

"We have to leave our shoes by the door," Ethan said, his voice whispery and light, as if he had just delivered the punch line of a joke. "White," he added when he flipped on a lamp and pointed to the carpet.

Ethan placed his shoes against the wall behind the door. Jerry left his a little farther away, underneath a glass-topped table. Mrs. Moeller had not waited up to greet them, and Ethan pressed a finger to his lips as he led Jerry through the rooms of the apartment.

"You have to see the view," Ethan whispered, and walked to a wall of white curtains. He drew them open and unlocked a panel of sliding glass doors. Outside, on a large, glass-enclosed terrace, Jerry stood in his socks atop another soft, white carpet.

"See the monument?" Ethan said, and Jerry looked in the direction he pointed. The view was astonishing, an evening panorama of flickering lights.

"No," Jerry answered, following the deep-black gap of the Potomac toward a cluster of lights.

"The one with the red blinking light," Ethan said, and Jerry looked and then nodded.

Late in the night Ethan found Jerry lying on the floor of the carpeted terrace, staring at the view, his head propped up by a cushion from the sofa. Without a word Ethan stretched out behind him and wrapped his arms around Jerry's waist. Jerry felt Ethan's breath brush against the side of his neck as Ethan pulled their bodies tighter together. Jerry thought it odd how firm Ethan's grasp felt; usually Jerry was the one clutching and holding. He wondered if Ethan really did not want him to go. There, lying so close to one another, Jerry had smelled, in rapid succession, the odor of Ethan's hair and breath and skin. Jerry felt his strength, his detachment, chemically decomposing as the warmth of Ethan's body began to envelop him. He closed his eyes and imagined himself somewhere else, perhaps a bird flying above, taking in the entire view. But he was unable to keep his distance; Ethan kept shifting his grasp, and Jerry, wanting to know what he should be feeling, kept flying in closer and closer for some sort of sign.

This morning, when Jerry awoke still on the floor, Ethan was no longer beside him, and the view from the terrace had disappeared behind the falling snow.

o

"You're not at all what I imagined," Mrs. Moeller said when she first saw Jerry. Jerry was seated in a wicker chair on the terrace. Ethan was in the kitchen making breakfast. They had not yet begun to unload the van. Mrs. Moeller shuffled onto the terrace in furry pink slippers.

"I had hoped you'd be short, dumpy, and balding," she said, and jiggled the ice cubes in her cocktail glass as she walked. Jerry stood as she approached, but Mrs. Moeller turned her back on him abruptly, and pinched the top flaps of her pink bathrobe together with two fingers, as though shyly trying to conceal her breasts. Her shrug, so feminine and partial, made Jerry, in his sweatshirt, jeans, and work boots, feel awkward and out of place. He shoved his hands into the back pockets of his jeans, not knowing what else to do. A soft gray light filtered through the windows. Outside, snow was spinning furiously in currents of air.

"I bet it's even snowing in Miami," she said.

Mrs. Moeller was not what Jerry had envisioned either. He was surprised to find she was close to six feet tall, almost as tall as himself and Ethan. He had imagined a short, frail woman to match the thin, reedy voice he had heard on the phone for months, and would not have been disappointed to have found her plump and matronly. Instead, Mrs. Moeller stood steady and proud before the windows, and seemed not at all a woman who had just turned

72

seventy, or a woman who was continuously dying. Her eyes were tiny gray circles, and though she wore not a trace of makeup, her skin glowed at the crests of her cheekbones as though she had applied rouge. Her hair, dyed white and curled in long, thin waves, snaked around her head and disappeared beneath the collar of her robe.

Ethan entered the terrace carrying a tray of food: plates of omelets, toast, jelly, butter, milk, and orange juice.

"I can't eat that garbage," Mrs. Moeller yelled at Ethan as he placed the tray on the table in the corner of the terrace.

"I thought we'd eat out here," Ethan said calmly, and began arranging the table.

Mrs. Moeller turned again, abruptly toward Jerry, and spoke. "I don't know why I still buy that stuff. I can't eat eggs because of the cholesterol. I can't eat wheat bread because I'm allergic to it. When I drink milk it makes my stomach feel like a meat grinder."

"So why don't you just drink yourself into a stupor while we eat," Ethan said matter-of-factly.

Jerry almost laughed at Ethan's remark, but caught himself by coughing.

"Do you have a cigarette?" Mrs. Moeller asked Jerry.

"No," Jerry answered.

"Just ignore her," Ethan said.

"I hope you live to see the day your children abuse you," she screamed at Ethan.

"I don't intend to have children," Ethan replied.

"Then there is hope for the human race after all," she said. "At least we won't be overrun with whiny little faggots."

"Enough, Mother," Ethan said without raising his voice. "Did you take your pill?"

"I'm not supposed to drink when I take that thing," she said.

"That's the point," Ethan responded.

"It's like swallowing a hairbrush," she said to Jerry. She walked to the table and poured a swig of orange juice into her glass and then walked to the other side of the terrace to a liquor cabinet and opened a bottle of vodka.

"Did Ethan give you a tour?" Mrs. Moeller asked in a bright, little-girl intonation as she crossed to the other side of the terrace again, wobbling slightly as her slippers dug into the carpet.

"Yes," Jerry answered. "You have a beautiful apartment."

Mrs. Moeller leaned across the table and wiped a finger over the top of a stick of butter and then slipped her finger into her mouth.

"This apartment is the exact same size as the house. Only sixteen floors higher. I miss the house," she sighed, and sat down in one of the chairs. "I miss George and Fred and Dina. I even miss that damn dachshund I had." She twisted one hand around her other wrist as though adjusting a bracelet. "But I made sure I kept the view."

Last night, as they lay on the carpet watching the lights, Ethan had told Jerry his family had owned Montebello Hill for over a century. After his father died, his mother remarried and her second husband convinced her to build the condominium tower, but died of a heart attack before the construction was completed. As Jerry lay on the floor, listening to Ethan's story, Ethan slipped his hands beneath Jerry's shirt and gently began stroking the hair on Jerry's chest.

Mrs. Moeller stood and walked to the window again. "I can spend hours just watching. My grandfather used to keep horses in the north pasture." She cupped her elbow with the palm of her free hand and lifted her glass till it rested against her chin. Jerry thought he noticed her tilt her head slightly as she stared through the windows, as though she had found a passage through the obstruction of the snow and had paused, contentedly, at a view of her memory. "Now there's a Howard Johnson's there," she said. "You never have to change; the world will do it for you." She moved her hand through the waves of her hair and let it rest when it reached the side of her neck. "I can't feel a pulse," she turned and said to Ethan, but he ignored her, eating a slice of toast and reading the paper. "NOTHING!" she turned and screamed at Jerry. "NOTHING!"

Jerry, momentarily frightened and concerned, walked over to Mrs. Moeller and placed his hand against her neck. Her skin felt warm and damp, like a tea bag before it is thrown in the trash. "I can feel it," Jerry said.

Mrs. Moeller's face turned angry and she pushed his hand away. "What else do I have to tolerate?" she asked. She started to walk away but suddenly dropped to the floor, landing in a muffled thump on her knees; the glass and ice she held silently tumbled across the carpet. Instantly Ethan was out of his chair and knelt in front of her. Jerry stepped back, watching in horror. Ethan slipped his arms around his mother and kept her from falling completely over.

"I just want a cigarette," she whispered to Ethan.

She nestled her head against Ethan's shoulder and looked up at Jerry. "I live for the moments that I feel well."

o

Ahead, a portion of the highway was closed, and a man in a bright-orange parka waved the traffic toward a ramp. Ethan steered the van around the small windblown snow dunes and followed the cars to the top of the ramp. The snowing had stopped but the light which filtered through the steel-colored clouds was quickly fading; night had started etching the landscape with shadows. Through the window of the van, Jerry watched the highway disappear as they drove down a road and into the suburbs. He noticed, behind the houses which flashed into view, an open field blanketed by snow. As the road curved, the field burst into full view, and Jerry saw a group of children huddled together in the distance, at the top of a slope, bundled in bright coats and scarves, pushing each other to the bottom on sleds and metal trash-can tops.

On the other side of the field, a girl waving her red-mittened hands above her head distracted Jerry and he watched the ragged ends of her blue scarf bounce with her movements. When Jerry saw a tiny figure moving toward her, he realized the girl was a woman and the smaller figure a child. Briefly, Jerry thought of his own mother, and the way, when he had been a child, she would bend over him and her long, thin hands would lace up his boots.

Jerry's mother, like Mrs. Moeller, had that pure, pale, almost translucent skin. Jerry had inherited his father's Mediterranean complexion, and his father's height and agility and large-boned bulk. As a child Jerry had felt he was a source of disappointment to his parents. He stuttered, had dyslexia, and flunked second grade. At night, his mother, after drying her wet hands on her apron, would sit with him at the kitchen table and help him read aloud his assignments from school. When, at twelve, he suddenly began to grow, his father would take him every night to the park not far from the factory where he worked, and there taught Jerry how to dribble and shoot baskets. "It's your ticket out of here," Jerry's father had said, tossing a basketball between his palms. The day he left Pittsburgh on a college athletic scholarship, Jerry felt he had finally made his parents proud, but a few months later, when he returned home for a weekend, he sensed the disappointment again as he sat down at the kitchen table and announced that he was gay. His mother had bowed her head in shock and then started crying. His father had stood, confused, and left the room. Later, that night, his mother came into his bedroom and sat on the edge of the bed. She rubbed her hands together, as if they were still wet, placed them in her lap, and then calmly asked, "Who do we need to talk to to try to understand?" Now, miles away, riding in the van, he suddenly felt close to her, missed her, loved her.

At a stoplight, Jerry turned and noticed Ethan's profile and the way his fine blond hair fluttered in the wind which rushed in through a crack in the window. Ethan had the aloof good looks of the wealthy boy down the street, the kind someone could not help noticing and admiring, the kind with that smooth, hairless, athletic edge, and the remote, faraway gaze of a mannequin. Once, while waiting in line to see a movie, Jerry had thought Ethan, standing there, looked like a model he had noticed in a magazine, and then thought he and Ethan must seem such an unlikely couple, himself so different: dark, swarthy, almost ethnic-looking—working-class next to well-to-do. Matt, Ethan's lover before Jerry, had once said it was difficult for him to detect Ethan's moods: he was too easily distracted by Ethan's appearance. After months of living with Ethan, Jerry had finally learned how to judge Ethan's thoughts from the position of his eyebrows: raised, they might show surprise or excitement; angled, they could mean anxiety or anguish. Now Ethan's eyebrows were tensed toward the bridge of his nose, and Jerry knew that, though Ethan's concentration was on driving, his thoughts had escaped to another place.

Seven years ago Jerry met Ethan at a party in a loft in Cambridge. They had both recently graduated from college and settled in Boston. Jerry, dressed in a T-shirt and jeans, had been tending bar, pouring, stirring, and shaking drinks for a roomful of rowdy, overdressed men. When Ethan approached for a drink, Jerry looked up from a tray of lemon wedges he had been slicing and said, "Scotch and soda?"

"How did you know?" Ethan asked.

"Instincts," Jerry answered. "You can tell who drinks what after a while."

That night, Ethan waited and took Jerry home after the party. Though they had a few dates and occasional sex, the relationship that developed was one of friendship. Two months later, at a bar in Boston, Jerry introduced Ethan to Matt. Jerry and Matt had been roommates in college. Matt and Ethan became lovers. Two years ago, Matt made a doctor's appointment when he noticed a bruise near his ankle. Ten months later he was dead. One night, while sharing a cab after visiting Matt in the hospital, Jerry suggested that Ethan could move into the second bedroom of his apartment if necessary. It was a simple gesture of friendship; he knew Ethan had no necessity to move: no financial worries, no legal entanglements. Jerry had merely suggested the idea in case Ethan was afraid of being alone. Four months later Ethan moved in.

Jerry had always been aware that he and Ethan had become lovers out of need instead of passion. And he had been aware, too, that Matt's death had had a greater impact than initiating his relationship with Ethan. Now, having just reached thirty, Jerry found himself continually afraid: afraid of growing old, of living alone; afraid of illness and death, of telling Ethan how he felt about anything; afraid even of such silly things as aspirin, pork, and too much caffeine. When Jerry and Ethan began to live together, Jerry had felt layers of himself unfolding, as though an archaeologist had unearthed an ancient civilization. Jerry had spent years building up his defenses, assembling lists of things he liked and disliked doing by himself, knowing how to live alone without being lonely. But it had been an amazing thing for Jerry to come home from work and find Ethan cooking or exercising or playing the piano. Though he had had a string of boyfriends, Jerry had never had a lover. And as an only child, he had not had a roommate since Matt in college. Slowly, Jerry had come to rely on Ethan to be there, and the briefest, most unexpected thing could make Jerry instantly and profoundly happy. Then once, not long ago, at another party in Cambridge, Ethan was laughing and talking with a friend and said in a casual manner that Jerry had inherited him from Matt. Jerry, who stood beside Ethan, was struck with a sudden discomfort. He knew but had never recognized that in loving Ethan he was also loving the memory of Matt.

Jerry had met Matt his freshman year in college. In the last row of psychology class, Matt would create puzzles and quizzes and hand them to Jerry to solve. After class, Matt would suggest how Jerry should cut his hair, what clothes he should buy, and how they should be worn. Jerry smoked his first joint with Matt; Matt took Jerry to his first gay bar. Jerry felt Matt's friendship was a carnival that could never end. Matt was *always* there, his every idea full of inspiration. Matt improvised their summers at the beach and supervised their late-night trials with Quaaludes and speed. It surprised Jerry, then, one night last week, when Ethan said Matt had thought it odd that everyone expected him to lead the way, when in fact, he had confessed to Ethan shortly before his death, he felt he had been a poor guide.

Ethan slowed the van and shifted to a lower gear, approaching an icy turn with deliberate caution. Jerry placed his hand against the dashboard for balance. It seemed remarkable to Jerry that there was nothing in the expression on Ethan's face to suggest that he had once loved Matt. The only time Jerry remembered Ethan crying was the night Matt died. Ethan and Jerry had been sitting on the couch, waiting for the police and the coroner to arrive, when Ethan had suddenly leaned his head against Jerry's shoulder and begun crying. Jerry, instinctively, had put his arms around Ethan and pulled him tightly against his chest. Months later it occurred to Jerry that Ethan must have transferred his depression to Jerry that night, as though his tears, seeping through the T-shirt Jerry wore, had moistened and weakened Jerry's heart. Now, in the van, Jerry could feel only the cold air and a vacant space in his chest. Ethan turned onto an empty street but accelerated too quickly, and the rear of the van skidded across a patch of ice and drifted, politely, into a bank of snow.

o

"What the hell?" Mrs. Moeller screamed. A loud thud had rocked one of the terrace windows.

"A bird," Ethan said, and was instantly beside the window. "It must have been a bird."

Jerry joined them at the window, though the view before him resembled static on a giant TV screen. "I've never seen a bird fly in the snow," he said.

"The world is ending," Mrs. Moeller remarked, and padded across the carpet to the liquor cabinet.

Ethan ran his hand down Jerry's back, and Jerry felt him pause and slip a finger around a belt loop of his jeans. Jerry turned away from the window so that Ethan's gestures were hidden from his mother, and then twisted his own hand around Ethan's. Ethan lifted their hands underneath the back of Jerry's sweatshirt, still damp from moving boxes this morning. Jerry felt their hands relax and heat the cool, wet spot at the center of his lower back. The touch reminded Jerry of the mornings, after showering, when he would shave in front of the mirror, and how Ethan would place his hand on Jerry's back as he edged his way around the tiny bathroom they shared. At first Jerry was worried Mrs. Moeller might react violently to their public affection, but in the passion of the moment he decided he wouldn't care. Mrs. Moeller had changed into a sky-blue satin kimono, and her hair was concealed beneath a bright-red wig, her complexion now powdered to match the color of the snow.

"I thought your hair used to be light brown," Mrs. Moeller said to Jerry. She weaved as she paced around the terrace, and her words had begun to slur together. "Did you dye it?"

"That was Matt, Mother," Ethan said without flinching.

"Matt?" his mother questioned, and pouted her lips at Ethan. "I can't remember anything I've done in a day." She looked at Jerry. "Tomorrow I won't even remember you." She walked away and sat on the sofa. "What ever happened to Matt?" she asked, and twirled a finger through her cocktail.

"He's dead," Ethan answered, and stroked Jerry's skin with the tips of his fingers.

She squinted her eyes. "Was it quick and painless?"

"No," Ethan replied. "For once, Mother dear, you don't have a monopoly on pain."

"Pity," she said, and placed her hand on her breast. "Nothing seems real except the pain. If my son had been a doctor instead of a faggot, maybe I wouldn't feel it so much."

Jerry felt his body flush with indignation, and would have shouted an obscenity and left the room had Ethan not unraveled their grasp and yelled at his mother, "What have I done to make you feel so ashamed of me?"

"It's disgusting what two men will do to each other," she yelled back.

"It's not what they do together that disgusts you, Mother,"

Ethan said, his voice more composed but still exasperated. "It's what they feel together that really disgusts you. You were the same way with Dina after she got married. You couldn't stand seeing someone happy when you weren't. Sometimes I regret I was never what you wanted me to be. But what makes you think I was born to save the world, or, better yet, born to save you from the world? Why do I feel you're trying to blame me because you found out one day Dad didn't love you anymore?"

"I never understood," she sighed, and rattled the ice cubes in her glass. "Turn on the radio. Maybe the world will cheer us up."

o

It took almost an hour to get the van out of the bank of snow. Jerry shredded old newspapers and gathered twigs and placed them under the wheels, rocking the van with as much strength as he could find while Ethan kept shifting from first to reverse. The van would lurch forward but the rear wheels would spin futilely, sending gray-colored slush into the evening sky like fireworks. Finally, with the help of two men from a nearby house, they pushed the van back onto the street.

Last night, as they lay on the floor, Ethan had slipped Jerry's clothes off and slowly begun massaging and kissing Jerry's body. Jerry, too, had undressed Ethan, and the sensation of their skin rubbing together had been magically electric. Jerry felt that perhaps it was the first time he had captured Ethan's passion since that first night, years ago, in Cambridge, when their sex had had such a raw, anonymous edge. But later, deeper in the night, Ethan, his head resting on Jerry's chest, had said, "You know, Jerry, I *do* love you." Jerry, once again trying to soar high above the room, had felt Ethan's voice resonating through his body.

"I'm sorry," Jerry said when they were driving again.

Ethan turned and gave Jerry a quick, confused look. "It wasn't your fault. You can't apologize for the snow."

"No," Jerry answered. "About your mom."

Before they left to drop Jerry off, Jerry had said to Ethan's mother, "I told him he shouldn't do this. I don't want him to do this. And he doesn't have to do this. Maybe you won't remember me, but I hope you'll at least remember that this is his choice." Jerry had no intention of hurting Mrs. Moeller, and he did his best to hide his anger and sorrow beneath a soft, restrained voice.

Mrs. Moeller narrowed her eyes and Jerry noticed a flicker of discomfort, then, briefly, regret. "I don't know why I hate you so," she said. "I don't know why you hate me. Are we enemies because we both love my son?"

When they reached the Arlington Bridge, Jerry looked up through the windshield and saw the red blinking lights of the Washington Monument. They drove through the city in silence, and Jerry thought it strange the world could seem so peaceful simply because it was buried beneath layers of snow. He turned again and looked at Ethan. Sometimes it embarrassed Jerry to realize how many years he had spent thinking of Ethan as a friend or like a brother, and, now, how he had come to understand he had always loved Ethan differently, more urgently, than anyone else in his life. On Connecticut Avenue, Ethan pulled the van over to the curb and stopped. Jerry tapped his feet against the floor of the van and felt the cold and the melted snow biting its way through his boots. He flexed his toes to see if they were wet. Ethan leaned his head against the top of the steering wheel.

Jerry was upset, unable to leave the car. At times he had felt that Ethan had spent years pushing him away. He wanted, now, some concrete reason why their relationship had never worked: was it the way he looked, the way he moved, the way he had been raised, or perhaps, even, his thick, cumbersome voice?

"I'm scared," Ethan said, still clutching the steering wheel.

Jerry looked through the side window of the van, not wanting to wonder if Ethan still knew how to cry.

"My doctor wants me to start AZT next week."

"I'll come down if you want me to," Jerry replied, and clutched the bag beside him on the seat.

"Not yet," Ethan answered.

"I don't feel right leaving you," Jerry said.

"We'll still see each other."

"I know. But it's not the same."

"Jerry," Ethan whispered. "Don't make this more difficult."

"You never gave me a chance," Jerry said, and opened the door of the van, and the rush of cold air felt as bitter as heartbreak. In a few weeks Mrs. Moeller would find out Ethan was sick. In a year she would bury him beside her two husbands. Jerry twisted his feet toward the door, crouched, and balanced himself on the ledge of the van. As he jumped toward the curb he felt he had thrown himself into space, till he grasped the image of Mrs. Moeller kneeling on the floor, her arms curled around Ethan like a madonna cradling her child. He landed quietly and reluctantly in the snow, turned, and closed the door of the van without saying goodbye. Years from now he knew he would remember this moment: the pain of his feet sinking in the snow, treading with desperation to find the stability of the cement; the sound of the branches of the trees snapping and crackling from the weight of the ice; the stale, wet smell of the wool scarf he wore around his neck; and the dry, ashen taste which hovered in the back of his throat. Jerry knew he had to respect Ethan's decision; had fate dealt the cards differently, he, too, might have returned home. The light from a street lamp shivered across the snow. At the subway entrance, the last thing he noticed before heading underground was a digital clock atop a building across the street, blinking from 7:48 to 7:49.

WEEKENDS

ONE WEEKEND THREE YEARS AGO RANDY AND I DROVE TO THE mountains to scatter my brother's ashes at a park not far from where Randy now lives. My brother, Greg, and Randy had been lovers for almost ten years. The day Randy and I drove to the mountains the weather was sunny, an early-spring morning; forsythia and dogwood were blooming along the sides of the highway, but a raw edge of winter still lingered in the breeze. Randy and I were oblivious to it all, the sunshine and the spring; we sat silent and sullen and tired, weighed down by my brother's death and the enormity of our sorrow. I remember that what few conversations we were able to have that day were silly and dull, rotating around the color of my hair, the new shirt Randy was wearing, the perfume I had spilled while fumbling through my purse. I remember that day was full of blank thoughts and magnified sounds:

the noise of passing trucks, the thunder of an overhead jet, the annoying rattle of the glove-compartment door.

This morning Randy is in the kitchen of the farmhouse he rents with his new lover, DJ. The kitchen, small and renovated, is crammed with dark wooden cupboards and shelves; copper pots and pans are suspended from rafters. Weaving between Randy's feet are a drooling cocker spaniel and a brown tabby cat. Above, hanging in a cage near the window, two yellow parakeets are wildly cheeping. Everyone, it seems, is hungry, and Randy, confident and charismatic as a magician, deftly opens bags and cans and boxes and jars with a flourish for his enraptured audience. Burly and broad-shouldered, Randy lunges around the kitchen, placing dishes and pans and plates on the floor and counters so everyone will have food at the same time. Dressed in jeans, blue flannel shirt, and black work boots, Randy seems bulky and massive to me, so out-of-place in this compact kitchen, I half expect him to leave any minute to go outside to chop wood or tune the car or mow the grass. Instead, he leans over the bright-red high chair where Sara, an eleven-month-old baby, is seated, and poises a spoon full of strained pears before her pouting lips. Sara squirms and turns her head away. "Oh, eat a spoony for Auntie Laurie," Randy says, cooing in a high-pitched tone. "Show her what a good girl you are." Sara dips her head and bangs her hands on the high-chair tray. She gurgles and reaches for her bottle of apple juice with gimme-gimme fingers. Randy hands her the bottle and looks at me and shrugs. "So I give her what she wants? Does that make me a bad parent?" Sara, half Hispanic and half black, has eyes so dark the whites look blue. Randy and DJ have had Sara for three weeks; they found her at the hospital in Philadelphia where DJ used to work. Sara has AIDS; her mother died a month after she was born. When Sara was five months old she almost died of pneumonia, the same kind that killed my brother when he was thirty-one.

Spring arrives later in this region of Pennsylvania than it does in Philadelphia; this morning white misty clouds hide the slopes of the mountains, and I think I can smell the wet soil and pine needles through the cracks of the kitchen walls. Outside the window, I notice everything seems lost behind a fine white mist; it reminds me of the nebulous condition of my own mind. Since I arrived last night I have spent most of my time watching Randy and DJ watch Sara and their domesticated zoo. Sara, unable to sleep because of a cough, kept the household awake and attentive and pacing all through the night. The dog chased the cat and the cat stared at the birds. DJ, exhausted, disappeared an hour ago to shower and sleep. Randy, energized by another cup of coffee, has decided it is time to change Sara's diaper. As he slips on plastic gloves, I pull a clean diaper from the hamper beside the refrigerator. I slip my finger between the plastic lining and the white cottony material; it feels thin and grainy inside and reminds me of the gauze Randy used to press against the hole in Greg's chest.

In the year since I last saw Randy I have had a miscarriage and separated from my husband, Bert. I don't think one is related to the other, but I think I had expected a baby to hold Bert and me together a little while longer.

Last night, when I pulled into the driveway, Randy flipped on the porch lights and met me at my car. We hugged and kissed and smiled at each other in the cool night shadows. He led me into the house and introduced me to Sara. Within seconds she had been placed in my arms. Before I could even ask anything about her or DJ, Randy gripped my shoulder and asked, "But how are *you?*"

Bert, my ex-husband, is marrying again. The woman he is marrying is a girl of eighteen. Bert is thirty-eight. The day Bert phoned and told me his plans, I felt as if my head had been severed from the rest of my body. A pain shot behind my eyes and pulsed across my forehead. It was the first time I had cried since deciding on the divorce. And it was the first time I ever felt like hurting someone myself. I called Randy that day, just to hear the sound of his voice. "He used you, Laura," Randy said. "Now let him go." Randy had never liked Bert. Neither had Greg. But they never complained to me about him any of the years we were together. I married Bert so that he could obtain his American citizenship. Bert is Irish and part of an underground movement to free Northern Ireland. Three days after our wedding, Bert began traveling across the country, trying to raise money for his organization.

o

"I don't understand all the politics," DJ says, looking out through the kitchen window. He has arisen from his nap and his hair, wet when he fell asleep, now stands up in thick, black clumps.

"What I don't understand is the heterosexual logic," Randy adds.

"Hormones," I answer. "But I don't think it's mid-life crisis."

"They probably met while making bombs," Randy says.

"He's not a terrorist," I say.

"You don't have to defend him," Randy adds. "We're on your side."

DJ goes to Sara, lifts her off the floor, and cradles her in his arms. DJ, short and pudgy-looking in his dark-purple sweats, looks almost comic holding Sara, like a beat cop who has rescued a waif.

"I'm not fighting him," I say.

"You ought to report him to the FBI," Randy says, running an empty sock across the floor to amuse the cat.

"You mean the CIA," DJ says. "Aren't they international?" He picks up a Mickey Mouse rattle and shakes it in front of Sara's face. She reaches for it with her tiny fingers.

"I just want to move on," I answer.

"I never knew what you saw in him," Randy says. "He had the worst manners of anyone I ever met."

"He loved me," I answer, startled by my own abrupt answer. "There was a time I know he really loved me."

Randy remains silent. DJ turns his face down to Sara and blows her a kiss. Suddenly I can't seem to shake the image of Bert in bed with another woman. I look first at Randy and then at DJ, bobbing Sara up and down in his arms. Randy senses my sinking and tosses the sock in the air for me to catch. The cat, alarmed, jumps so wildly in my direction that it makes me laugh.

"He wasn't good enough for you," Randy says. "And you were too good to him."

o

Three years ago, when Randy and I scattered Greg's ashes, I thought I would probably never see Randy again. This weekend I am reminded how even now our lives keep interweaving. Randy met DJ in the hospital when Greg was dying; DJ was a nurse's aide who worked the ward in the mornings. DJ would visit my brother every day, bringing him the newspaper and helping him shave or shampoo his hair. Randy says he has few memories of DJ at that time; all he seems to remember is his own horror and rage. I remember that DJ showed up at Greg's funeral, sat beside Randy, and offered to take him home after the service.

"I know a doctor you could date," DJ says to me now. He is sitting cross-legged on the floor, helping Sara stack brightly colored rings. "Or, if you don't want to date him, he could get you a lot of drugs."

"Who?" Randy asks, alarmed. He turns the water off where he

had been rinsing dishes, wipes his hands on a dish towel shoved in his back pocket, and looks at DJ. "Who are you talking about?"

"Dr. Clayton," DJ says.

"Clayton? Do I know him?" Randy asks.

"No," DJ answers, and then turns toward me. "I saw him when I was trying to dry out, but he kept giving me prescriptions."

"He sounds like a real catch," Randy says sarcastically.

"Oh, he was so gorgeous," DJ adds, and I notice his eyes widen. "It was harder giving him up than the drugs."

"Laura needs someone nice," Randy says. "Not another jerk."

"What kind of drugs did you do?" I ask, moving my chair away from the kitchen table so I can get a better look at DJ.

"What *didn't* I do!" he says. "I went from booze to drugs to acid back to booze. Those years went by so fast. It's so hard for me to imagine it now. I was a totally different person." He helps Sara grab a yellow ring. "Didn't you ever have another life?" he asks, looking around the floor.

"Like Shirley MacLaine?" Randy yells from the sink.

"No, you know, like you did something you could never believe you could have ever done in your entire life if you had been able to sit down in advance and plan it all out. Or like one day you just wake up and say to yourself, 'Who is this?' or 'What is this?' or 'What the hell is going on?' "

There is another awkward silence and I am aware we are all thinking of Bert.

"Sex," Randy says, a little too pensively, and then looks at me. "Sex is always the hardest part to let go."

o

These are the facts: I married Bert because he saved my brother's life in a boating accident when Greg was on vacation in Ireland. My brother asked me to marry Bert. Our marriage was only planned to be a temporary arrangement. I never thought I would fall in love with him. Bert never said he would be faithful to me. But he also lied to me when he said he had no interest in other women. The girl he is marrying is a friend of his family in Ireland.

The hours pass and I absorb myself into Randy's world.

DJ and I do laundry, take a break to play Frisbee, and then sweep the garage. I help Randy vacuum the bedrooms, then talk to the parakeets while he begins to cook dinner. DJ takes me into his bedroom and cuts my wavy brown hair into a short, boyish cut. All of us—DJ, Randy, Sara, and the dog—take a walk after dinner to look at the ruins of the old Shaker meetinghouse not far down the road.

Later that night, after a game of charades, Sara, DJ, and the animals fall easily asleep, and Randy and I are alone in the living room, drinking wine and listening to *La Bohème* on the stereo.

"Remember the weekend I spent with you and Bert?" he asks me.

"I remember," I answer. "You were such a mess."

"I was practically comatose. I remember I couldn't move from the couch. All I wanted was to be in the middle of someone else's world. I remember Bert trying to get me to go to the store with him. I nearly pitched a hissy fit because I had to put my shoes on." Randy laughs, more of a chuckle to himself. "It gets easier," he says, and though I am not looking at him, I imagine I hear his sigh.

"I know," I answer.

"I didn't love DJ at first," Randy says. "And I hate dogs and cats and especially chirpy little birds. Babies scare me to death. But I had to put all the pieces together to keep from dwelling so much on Greg. I had to have something to do."

I turn and watch him slip his hand behind his head. "I even

hate opera," he adds. "But I listen to it, because it fills up all the empty spaces."

"I know," I answer, feeling the sudden rush of the wine through my body. I refill our glasses and then place the bottle of wine on the floor, a little too awkwardly, and watch the bottle totter as if in slow motion. For a moment I want it to roll over and spill on the floor, just so I can get up, so I can have something else to clean.

"To someone old and something new," Randy says.

"To something borrowed and someone blue," I reply.

o

When Greg was alive I spent a lot of time with him and Randy. Greg and I were twins; I was born two minutes and seventeen seconds before him. Because I was older, I felt very protective of him. Greg always believed it was because we thought alike. When we were children Greg and I shared almost everything: birthday parties, haircuts, and pony rides. For years I considered myself half boy, half girl. I went hunting and fishing with Greg, played baseball, and collected insects. Growing up, Greg and I told each other everything. Greg taught me how to fight. I showed him there was nothing wrong with crying. He stayed home with me the day I had my first period. Greg told me he thought he was gay long before he ever slept with another guy. I always wanted with Bert the sort of relationship I had with Greg.

Tonight, three years after Greg's death, it is dark and late and even Randy has now fallen asleep. This weekend I have been thinking a lot about Greg to keep from thinking too much about Bert. Both, I recognize now, hurt equally as much, though in different, aching, painful ways. Sometime this weekend I expected some sort of catharsis, perhaps a cleansing of anything that has to do with Bert. But I am smart enough, I think, to know that it is not going to be possible. Strands of Bert will always be woven into my life. The way to deal with it now, I guess, is to keep myself distracted. I find my sweater and decide to take another walk to see the meetinghouse ruins, this time by moonlight, this time alone except for the sounds of the country night.

In the morning, before I leave to drive back to the city, DJ finds his camera and follows me outside to the car. It is sunny but cool, one of those brilliant, crisp spring mountain mornings. We spend a few minutes taking pictures. Me with DJ, me with Randy, Randy and DJ, DJ and Sara, even the dog joins us for a couple of poses. As I am about to leave, DJ says, "Wait, one last picture with you and Sara by the car." I hold Sara in my arms and walk into a patch of sun in front of my car.

As DJ lifts the camera to his face I notice Randy on the lawn, approaching us, lifting his hand to his forehead and brushing his scalp with his knuckles. Momentarily, as quick as a snapshot, Randy and I stare at one another as though we've both seen a ghost. I realize, here, in the sunlight, dressed in jeans and with my new short haircut, I look perhaps a bit too much like Greg, and Randy's gesture with his hand is something Greg always did. Randy and I look away from one another, back again, and then once more away. He approaches and hugs me, somehow Sara ends up in DJ's arms, the weekend is over, and I am back in my car headed toward Philadelphia.

o

Months later Sara is dead, and Randy shows me a copy of the photograph when he visits me in Philadelphia. We spend the weekend talking about DJ, Greg, Bert, Sara, even the dog and the cat and the parakeets suspended above his kitchen window.

Randy mentions he wants to adopt another baby. I show Randy the new office where I work. We laugh, cry, eat, and drink lots of wine together. Monday morning the weekend is over; Randy helps me with the dishes and says he feels better. Then he leaves, eager to see DJ and the mountains again.

WHAT YOU
TALK ABOUT

Y OU HAVE MADE ARRANGEMENTS TO MEET HIM AT A BAR. HE IS
a friend of a friend. When you talked on the phone with him, he
seemed nice and interested in you, but you were hesitant about
meeting him for a date. In the last two years, you have had only
two other blind dates; one was bald and the other wore an earring
in his left ear. Not that this really bothered you; you have dated
men before with both those characteristics. But the first one had
the mannerisms of a truck driver and the appearance of a nerd,
the second looked like the type of person you would avoid in dark
alleys. And what really did bother you was you could not connect
with them no matter how hard you tried; they were both so vague,
one was even mysterious. But when your friend from Chicago
called last week to see how you were doing, he said, I know
someone you might want to meet. You told your friend that you
hated blind dates, and reminded him of your previous ones, the

bald guy and the man with the earring. Your friend answered rather emphatically, I think this is someone you might want to meet. He only lives forty-five minutes from you.

You are meeting this blind date at a bar you have never been to. It is a bar attached to a restaurant. Your expectations are not high and you are a little stressed out from a tough week at a job you don't much like. It is Friday night. You are only doing this because of your friend from Chicago, because he keeps hounding you to start dating again, to start seeing someone. Sometimes your friend, who still lives in Chicago, doesn't seem to comprehend that there are not many available gay men who live in this area of Indiana.

The arrangement you made with this blind date was only for a drink; dinner together following was an option either party could refuse. However, you are already hungry. As you enter the bar, you hope for a moment you have been stood up.

There are only two men in this bar. One you estimate is over sixty-five. You know it is not him. In the light of this bar, which is dim, the other man looks quite handsome: virile and rugged, like the type riding a horse in a cigarette ad. You try to wipe the shock from your face as he turns to you and speaks your name.

You wonder how he recognized you. You worry a minute about whether you look too gay as he shakes your hand; after all, this is a straight bar. Then you remember you told him you wore black wire-rim eyeglasses. No one else in the bar is wearing black wire-rim eyeglasses.

As he rises from the bar stool where he was seated, you see he is shorter than you expected. Though he told you he was six feet tall, he does not seem four inches taller than you. Perhaps it is because he told you he weighed 165 and you thought that he would be skinny. This six-foot guy looks healthy, you notice. He has a full head of hair and no earring. You observe right away that he has large hands and small feet. You sit down on a bar stool and worry because you think your feet are larger proportionally than your hands. He sits down beside you and places his hand against his beer bottle. You order a beer, even though it has been months since you've had any alcohol.

There is an awkward pause after your first sip of beer. The carbonation in your mouth and stomach has jolted your senses. You cough and look at the bartender, a short, husky man with closely cropped black hair peppered with gray, and admire the way the tendons of his arms flex as he wipes the inside of a glass with a cloth. You think that the bartender is not better-looking than this guy. Your blind date asks if you had any trouble finding the bar. No, you answer, only finding a parking space on this block. You ended up parking on a side street. There is another awkward pause. You look around the bar and say this is a nice place, you never knew it existed. He says he has been here only a few times and points to a doorway that leads to the restaurant. He says it is rather expensive. Another awkward pause and he asks you how your week was. A strange question to ask, you think, because at the beginning of this week he did not even know you. Rough, you answer, and begin to complain about the woman you work for and the hour it takes to commute to your job. You start to describe your car, an old relic, which you are convinced personally dislikes you because it keeps having to be repaired, when you realize you are complaining too much. You ask him how his day was, but your voice sounds edgy. It doesn't sound as sincere as when he asked his question. While he tells you he got up early this morning to finish a few errands and do some cleaning before leaving for work, you notice he sounds calm, as though all his thoughts are carefully organized before he speaks. His voice is light and fluid; you cannot detect any accent. When you mention you saw a tiny field mouse run across your bathroom carpet this morning he laughs, and you like the way it ends in a quick, raspy crack. He says he was busy at work and adds he got home around four o'clock and took a nap before coming here tonight. No wonder he seems so at ease, you think. No wonder he looks so good. No wonder he doesn't look bitter, angry, or depressed. He had a nap.

What you know about him already: He told you he does not smoke or do drugs. He is a teacher. Like you, he is in his early thirties and he is looking for a friend and/or lover. He likes to go bowling and refinish furniture and considers himself conservative. During the first phone conversation you had with him, he told you he has a cat, lives in a third-floor apartment, doesn't go out to bars much unless with a friend, and was reading *Significant Others* when you called. Enough to convince you he was not an ax murderer.

You ask him what subject he teaches. He says botany. You ask if that is a requirement for a high-school diploma in this state. He answers that it is a special course for advanced students. While he is explaining the course he teaches, you are thinking about the house you are renting. You had heard that the previous tenants were amateur horticulturalists. In your yard, there are several plants surrounded by wire or propped up by long, thin stakes. You wonder how to work this into the conversation. You don't when you realize you don't know the names of any of these plants, and you are attracted to this guy, he interests you, and you don't want to turn him off by seeming ignorant.

He asks you if you grew up in Indiana. You tell him you are originally from the South and after college you moved to Chicago, where you lived for twelve years. You say you never even realized this state existed until you visited last summer with a friend whose

parents live in a nearby city. You tell him you have lived in Indiana
for only three months. The only people you know are your friend
from Chicago, who occasionally visits his parents, the real-estate
agent who rented you your house, and a lesbian couple who run
a hotel nearby. You don't mention the reason you moved out of
Chicago. You don't mention that everything about the city was
beginning to annoy you; your job made you irritable. You say
nothing about your lover dying from AIDS. You don't mention
that after the funeral there was nothing else for you to do in the
city and so you had a nervous breakdown. You only say you needed
a change. You try to keep the conversation light. You tell him it
is so different living in a rural area. You mention you just learned
how to clean your chimney. You add you never realized you would
spend so much time scraping frost off your windshield.

He tells you he has lived here for three years. Before that he
was in North Carolina and Pennsylvania and California. He asks
you if you have dated much. You wonder what the term *date*
means this year and in this part of the country. Does it mean date
as in getting together with a friend, date as in one person pays
for everything two people do, or date as it was known in the
seventies, to have sex? You opt for the last choice, since he is your
age, and you realize your answer really fits all three definitions:
not much.

You notice he is staring at you. Looking you over. You think
at last all those mornings you spend exercising are finally paying
off. You know you look younger than your stated age. All your
friends tell you so, tell you that you could pass for someone in
his late twenties. You wonder if your date notices the tiny nick
in the cleft of your chin where you cut yourself shaving this
morning. He asks you if you drive to the bars in Chicago. You
say you did when you first moved here, because you missed the

city. But you don't anymore. You mention you watch a lot of movies on the weekends now.

He is wearing a heavy knit maroon sweater, but you can tell he keeps himself in shape by the way the fabric stretches across his shoulders. You imagine what he looks like undressed, though you cannot determine whether his chest is hairy or smooth. You decide it must be smooth, because you do not notice any hair at his wrists, and though you remind yourself you must be interested in the person, not the physique, you cannot shake the mental photograph you have created of the two of you in bed together, your head resting on top of his smooth chest. You wonder if he likes to kiss, cuddle, wrestle, or massage. He looks briefly at you and then glances in the direction of the bartender. You know he is making a comparison. He turns again toward you and you study his expression, looking for some sort of sign of disappointment, but he smiles at you and takes a sip of his beer. You wonder what sex would be like with him. Is he rough or passionate, gentle or affectionate? You begin to twirl the bottom of the beer bottle between the palms of your hands, a habit you have when you are nervous. You wonder if he knows what you are thinking. You wonder when was the last time he had sex. You wonder if he would be afraid to kiss you.

When you spoke with him on the phone you told him you are hardworking and honest, stable but shy, which is why you are never relaxed at a bar. You said you are easily entertained and consider yourself a romantic. You mentioned you are both rational and adventurous, intelligent and athletic, and have a dry, sometimes cynical sense of humor. You said you like traveling, reading magazines, and playing the piano, enjoy the theatre, photography, and biking. You told him you watch your weight, eat plenty of fiber, and keep your light-brown hair short and trimmed regularly. You added you are a casual dresser, choosing clothes for comfort, though tonight you are wearing the indigo shirt that makes your eyes look softer, bluer. You notice you are both wearing jeans, though his are a new blue and yours are an old black. You make a mental note of what you are wearing. If you see this guy again you must not wear the same outfit.

He asks you if you went home for the holidays. You say no, because you were just there in September for your younger sister's wedding. You say this matter-of-factly, without any emotion. You think your tone sounded a little too blunt, so you add that your parents' house in Memphis was too far to drive to with only one day off, so you spent the holiday with your friend and his mother. There is an awkward pause. You notice his expression, which you think looks serious. You think this is too much information for him to register at once. Then he says his sister is expecting a baby any time now. She lives in Florida, and he explains his mother spent the holidays down there this year. You think a moment about Florida and the sun and the beach and the hot weather.

Something else you remember you know about him already. His lover died of AIDS three years ago, roughly about the time your lover became sick. For a moment you wonder how he handled it; you wonder if he had a breakdown, like you.

You ask him if he thinks it is going to snow this weekend. He says they are predicting four to six inches. You remember you have just spent a fortune to have snow tires put on your car. You ask him how the roads are here when it snows. He says they are pretty good about plowing the main ones, but the back roads can be difficult.

You have finished your beer. He takes the last sip of his. He asks if you want to have dinner. He's interested, you think, and you answer yes. He asks where you want to eat. You remember you don't have a lot of money in your wallet. You suggest a place three blocks away, a restaurant that has a comfortable, homey feel: dark, nonpretentious, and inexpensive. You slip on your jacket and head for the door.

Outside, you walk slightly ahead of him. The sidewalk is narrow, and since you are the one who knows where the restaurant is, you lead the way. When you arrive at the building, you hold the door open for him to enter first. Inside, you watch him mentally take in the surroundings.

A blond waiter shows you to a table. Looking at the menu, your blind date asks you what you recommend. You say the chicken and veal are good, but you will probably order something light, like the chef salad. You think to yourself that this appears healthy, and when you ordered it once before, you couldn't finish it. You don't want to appear piggish.

The waiter brings glasses of water and takes your order. Your blind date opts for the chicken. You stick with the salad. When the waiter leaves, your date asks if you think the waiter is cute. You say, sort of, and mention that if he had shaved and showered this morning, he could probably be a knockout. He says he has a weakness for blonds. You feel like you've lost a race. You wonder what you would look like if you dyed your hair.

The lighting is brighter in the restaurant than it was at the bar. You notice for the first time your blind date has brown eyes. There is a small bend at the bridge of his nose. You wonder if it was ever broken. You want to ask him to come over tonight. Instead you ask him what his plans are for the weekend.

He tells you he has some work to do on Saturday and then adds he is having brunch on Sunday with some friends. He asks if you like to cook. You answer, only if it's frozen. You have little patience for chopping, stirring, browning, and all that stuff. He says he enjoys cooking. You think he holds the invention of the microwave against you. He asks what type of food you like to eat. You say, just about anything, but your all-time favorite food is pineapple upside-down cake. He says he likes vegetables a lot. What type of vegetables do you like? he asks. You feel an urge to roll your eyes but you suppress it. Again you feel defeated. You are thirty-four years old and you are being judged by your interest in vegetables. Anything, you answer. Except lima beans. You wrinkle your nose. It is an ingrained reflex. You instantly regret your answer. There is only one other word in the English language which produces that same expression on your face and that word is *liver*. And though you don't mention that, you can't keep from thinking about it. He says he likes lima beans.

You try to redeem yourself by saying your mother was not a good cook. You explain to him how over the years you have developed a taste for things slightly charred. You know instinctively this conversation is headed in the wrong direction. There is an awkward pause. You panic that you have lost him. You change the subject. You ask him if he saw the new Bette Midler movie. He says he hasn't been to a movie in about four months. You are thankful when the waiter reappears with your food.

You talk sporadically while you eat. You offer him your onions, which he accepts. He offers you a taste of his chicken, which you decline because you are not in the mood for chicken. But then you worry he might be offended you didn't accept—you remember someone once told you sharing food is an intimate gesture—so you tell him you changed your mind, you will try a piece. You watch him slice off a corner of a thigh and place it on your plate. You wonder what it would be like sitting down to dinner every night with this man. Would you like what he cooks, would your plates match his glasses, could you afford to live in a place that has a built-in dishwasher? You wonder if he is neat or sloppy. Does he leave the cap off the toothpaste, forget to flush, wash colors and whites together, remember to take the trash out on Wednesdays? You hope he wouldn't object to your favorite towel, the old, unraveling, large dark-green one.

You have finished dinner and have ordered a cup of coffee, decaffeinated. You are frantically racking your brain so you can make some sort of connection with this man. He asks you what type of music you listen to. You say you enjoy everything except heavy metal. You tell him what you listen to is usually determined by your mood. You like oldies during the week, Top 40 and disco on Saturdays, and classical, preferably baroque, on Sundays. You also explain that you usually like a particular song more than an artist, which is why you haven't bought any albums in a long time. He says he likes country music a lot. You say you like the way country music has evolved over the last few years. The way the lyrics have matured. You say you like country music a lot more since you no longer live in the South. He says his favorite singer is Patsy Cline. You agree, Patsy Cline is unbeatable.

You split the bill and leave the waiter a generous tip, in spite of the fact he was a distracting blond. Outside, the night air feels refreshing and you walk together in the direction of your car. You realize you have done too much talking and thinking tonight and you are tired. But nothing has been said about your lover who died, or his lover who died, yet you know you have both been thinking of both of them. You have mentioned nothing about drugs, insurance rates, or T-cell counts. He has said nothing about testing positive, though neither have you, but you know from your friend in Chicago that this is the simple, ineffable link you share with this man.

When you reach your car, you suddenly remember you have

never given him your phone number. You don't want to seem pushy about getting together another time. You want him to make the next move, to see if he is interested in you. At your car he asks if you want to get together again next week. You say yes and write your number on a piece of paper you find in your glove compartment. You hand him the paper and you both stand awkwardly on the sidewalk. You say, "It was nice to meet you, Carl." There is no attempt at a kiss; this is a small town after all. You shake hands and he says, "I'll call you soon, Robbie."

In the car, driving home, you wonder if he will ever call. You think again about Jay and miss him, deeply. And then you think again about vegetables. You wish you had told Carl you really like spinach. You have always liked spinach. You will always like spinach.

THE ABSOLUTE
WORST

STUCK IN TRAFFIC WAITING TO CROSS THE POTOMAC RIVER INTO
Virginia, Katie adjusted the rearview mirror so she could see Bryan
in the back seat of the car. She had not really kidnapped him; if
she were to be pulled over now by the police, she felt certain she
could explain it all in a simple, though stumbling, way. Bryan had
been in the hospital for over ten days, fighting first pneumonia,
then a viral infection, and then had been kept for more tests and
had developed another infection. Katie had asked Bryan's doctor,
a small perfunctory Asian man, if it would be possible to take
Bryan out of the hospital for a few hours one afternoon. "Absolutely
not," the doctor had replied. "Unheard of," another doctor answered. And when Katie tried to explain that she wanted to take
Bryan to see a friend who was now homebound, that she felt the
trip would only help Bryan, help both of them, the doctors stared

at her as though she were speaking a foreign language, a language they showed no interest in wanting to understand.

But Katie had been persistent. She had only recently discovered that Chris was living at his father's house. Not living really, she amended in her mind, *dying*. And she knew Bryan's spirits were slipping and she wanted, no, she *had* to bring Chris and Bryan together again; they had not seen each other in almost four years. She had discussed the possibility of the trip with a hospital administrator, an unyielding heavyset woman, who had assured her it could be medically done but had refused to allow Katie to do it. Katie had consulted with the interns and the nurses, mentioned it to the cafeteria staff, described it to visitors and even other patients, anyone who would listen to her. It had become the most important obsession in her life, but even deeper, more passionately, she felt that it was something that could keep both Bryan and Chris alive. This morning, while she was reading a magazine in Bryan's room, waiting for him to wake up, a nurse opened the door and said, "Just do it. We'll all cover for you. But you have to have him back in three hours."

Now Katie looked again in the mirror, trying to see how Bryan was holding up. His eyes were closed, as though he was sleeping. But was he sleeping or was he unconscious? She thought he looked distressed, as if blood were not passing through his face, and she had a sudden, horrible thought: what if he were to die here, in the car? Would she then be responsible for his death? Would that make her a murderer? He won't, she decided. Somewhere she had heard that if you think something hard enough, you can will it to happen. Or not to happen. He won't, he won't, he won't die. Not in the car. Not in *this* car. Then it occurred to her that maybe Bryan didn't even know where they were going, or wasn't even aware he was riding in a car. She had never discussed the trip with him, wanting to keep seeing Chris again as a surprise.

And then everything had happened so fast. A nurse had brought a wheelchair; a security guard had helped Bryan into the car. And Katie had been a rapid fire of questions. Should he eat? What should he drink? What happens if he passes out, vomits, his fever rises?

Why had she been so persistent? Wasn't this a foolish idea? Not even the weather had cooperated; a light drizzle painted the city with a November chill. Now she was stuck in traffic and reduced to a hysterical panic beneath a billboard for mint-flavored mouthwash. What is the worst that can happen? she thought. There must be something worse than this.

○

Things had begun to fall apart about three years ago, when Bryan met Katie at a coffee shop near Dupont Circle and said he had tested positive. Bryan had become again, at that point, a day-to-day part of Katie's life. They spoke on the phone, cooked dinner for one another, went shopping and to the movies together. That day Katie had watched Bryan's mouth move through words like "monitor" and "drugs," but the sentences fell apart, words shattered on the ground. All she could think was that *it* was now moving in closer, happening to her. Not that *it* had eluded her world before; she and Bryan had both known friends who had been diagnosed and had died. Bryan had also volunteered as a buddy for over a year and now worked on the switchboard on Thursday nights, the same night Katie delivered meals to homebound patients in her neighborhood. "It" was a subject that was, unfortunately, very commonplace in their lives. In fact, only a few weeks before, she had encouraged Bryan to get tested.

She knew the news wouldn't have hit her so hard if things in her own life had not started to unravel. Ellen, her lover, had finally left her and moved to Seattle. And Katie had immersed herself in support groups, twelve-step programs, and private therapy to try to stop drinking, to stop smoking, and to get out of the house and over the relationship. She felt her life had been reduced to tearful nights on the floor, floundering through spasms of misery, wanting a drink or a cigarette or Ellen to come back and say she had made a mistake. And now to all this she had to add the thought of Bryan possibly dying, when she felt he was the only thing she had left to make her go on.

She had stared at Bryan that day and thought he didn't look different. He did not seem depressed, sad, desperate. He was talking in a low, calm voice. But wasn't that the way Bryan always was? Cool, academic, rational? Then Bryan said that he was hesitant about mentioning all of this, because he knew it would set her back. *Set her back?* Of course it would; all she could think about was could she order alcohol at this restaurant, who could she bum a cigarette from, had Ellen left any Valium in the bathroom cabinet? But instead she had sat there and said, "Excuse me," and began to take deep breaths.

Bryan had flushed and became alarmed. "Are you all right?"

"Of course," she had answered in a tone she felt was too bitter. "I'm all right. I'm just trying to stay calm."

o

And then word came to Katie of other friends. Gene, a friend from high school, had developed cryptococcal meningitis. Darren, a co-worker, was now going blind from cytomegalovirus. Olivia, a woman in her support group, confided she had passed out after hearing the result of her lover's blood test. And then two of her homebound clients on Thursday nights died the same week. It got to the point where Katie could not answer the phone, could not watch TV, could not do anything to escape *it* except take long solitary walks through the darkened streets near Dupont Circle. But even that could not stop her from thinking. Or stop the infuriating need to drink or smoke. Every night, on her way home, she stopped and bought a donut or candy bar or an ice-cream cone—something, anything, to make her feel instantly better. And then she would say to herself, If I can just make it to the fall. If I can just make it to the end of the month, the end of the week, the end of tomorrow, everything will get better, *has* to get better.

Autumn came and went. Katie gained fifteen pounds. Some things *did* get better. But others became much worse.

o

The worst that can happen, Katie thought when she had parked the car in the driveway, is that Chris would not want to see Bryan. Or what if he couldn't see Bryan, what if Chris had developed a reaction to some drug and couldn't see at all? Or even worse, what if Chris had died since she had phoned the house from the hospital?

She opened the back door of the car and leaned inside, stirring Bryan awake. As she began to untangle a blanket from beneath him, she noticed the front door of the house open, heard the wood snap, and watched a young, red-haired girl, short and chunky, approach the car, parting the misty gray air like a torch.

"I'm Donna," the girl said, only now Katie could tell she was much older, a woman really, a few years older than herself. "We spoke on the phone. I help take care of Chris."

Donna leaned into the car and pressed her hand against Bryan's brow. "We have a wheelchair inside. Let me go get it."

Thank goodness she knows what to do, Katie thought. Thank goodness there is someone in charge.

Inside, Chris was sleeping, propped up in a large upholstered armchair in a wood-paneled den. Katie and Donna wheeled Bryan up beside the chair. Katie took a good look at Chris; if she hadn't known it was him, she would have never recognized him. His body was covered with small bluish lesions; his bones poked out from beneath his robe, like coat hangers suspending unworn clothing. She turned to Bryan, hoping that he might not have recognized Chris, that they could just leave before he realized who it was, but she detected the furious stare Bryan was already giving Chris. Unable to watch the horror fighting through Bryan's face, Katie turned away, toward the TV set, where a game show was playing without any sound. Donna reached for Katie's hand and said, "Let's leave them alone a bit."

This was the most foolish thing in the world to do, Katie thought as she followed Donna through the room. Bringing Bryan here, being here herself. She stopped and noticed, through the window, Chris' father, wearing a bright-orange parka, raking leaves into tiny brown mounds on the lawn.

"Mr. Pearson thought it best if he stayed out of the way," Donna said.

Katie turned and looked at Bryan again, watching him watching Chris sleep.

o

Katie believed they had begun their friendship by watching Chris. It was hard not to notice him their freshman year in college; Chris, with bushy black hair and bright-blue eyes, bounced around the campus in jeans and a bright-yellow sweatshirt, so illogical against the somber buildings of Georgetown. Bryan and Katie met when they realized they shared two classes together back to back— Biology 101 and Introduction to Western Civilization. Crisscrossing the campus in those days, they noticed Chris at the cafeteria, the bookstore, the library, his sweatshirt instantly identifiable. A few weeks later, they met at an audition for the campus choral group; Bryan and Chris had struck up a conversation about a group of guys who had eerily begun singing Gregorian chants in the basement of a dorm, and Katie, sitting between them, turned her head from side to side, not knowing what to say, but willing herself to be noticed, a part of their conversation.

Katie hadn't known they were gay in those days, or that Bryan and Chris were stumbling through those thoughts themselves at the time. But as she sat through more conversations on Broadway shows and MGM musicals, discussions about the harmonics of Chuck Mangione and The Manhattan Transfer, it occurred to her that something was happening between the two of them which she didn't understand. It came as no surprise a few months later when she listened to their heartfelt confessions of crushes on one another; she had already made the connection herself. And she felt both protector and protected as she began to explore a new world with them—a nightlife of bars and clubs and discos—a world that intrigued Chris, disheartened Bryan, and satisfied Katie, because it allowed her to learn to enjoy the company of gay men.

It came as no surprise to her either when Chris announced a year or so later that he and Bryan were now involved with one another, and would she be interested in sharing an off-campus apartment with them. The three of them traveled everywhere together—to the mall, to the beach, to New York to see a show—inseparable everywhere except in the bedroom. But Bryan and Chris never made Katie feel left out or like a third wheel; in fact, they relished her opinions as much as she did their confidences. They had even traveled to Europe together, renting a car the summer after graduation and driving from Paris to Rome and then back to Paris. By then Katie had also begun to silently question her own sexuality, aware that Bryan and Chris made her feel more attractive and special than the campus boys she had dated. She had even devised an explanation of her relationship with Bryan and Chris: they were, in her mind, her surrogate family.

So it did come as a surprise that after returning from Europe Bryan moved to New York to begin graduate school at Columbia and Chris stayed behind in Washington. Katie had been unaware that their relationship was splintering; there had been no tangible argument or misunderstanding. She was able to understand it only years later, looking back at the past. They had all been very different types of people who had been together at the same point in their lives and were now moving on to other points, becoming the people they were supposed to be, *wanted* to be.

Bryan began moving in more academic circles, began teaching college, and going to the opera, ballet, and Europe again. Chris floundered through a variety of jobs, hung out at the clubs and bars and gyms, then moved to New York himself and flirted with the idea of becoming an actor, before settling into a career in advertising. Katie took a job with a small publishing firm, then years later accepted a magazine assignment in New York, where she met Ellen. Still, Katie and Bryan and Chris came together every so often, for dinner, to celebrate a birthday, for a rendezvous at the beach, and though their differences had become more apparent and striking, it was still obvious they were happy when their lives could intersect, even for just a few hours.

Katie had once tried to explain all this to Ellen, how sometimes people move away to become other people, but that doesn't mean that they will never get along again, cannot still be friends. Ellen grew into an adamant and headstrong woman, however; she felt everyone should be, think, just as she did. Abused as a child, Ellen had always been mistrustful of men; she couldn't understand how Katie could feel comfortable in the company of men, even gay men. But, then, Ellen saw everyone as a potential threat; she could become jealous of even another woman's stray comment. Their relationship had begun at a time when Katie needed someone with a firm sense of direction. She had moved to a new city, begun a new job, and felt for the first time she had been misplaced. Ellen had wooed Katie with such urgency that her own sexual awakening came like a spiritual revelation. If Ellen had had her way, they would have joined a commune made up solely of lesbians. Instead they had compromised and moved to Washington, where Ellen began working as a lobbyist, growing angrier and angrier as she butted her head against the establishment. Katie returned to her old job at the publishing firm and soon became aware that what she needed from Ellen—wanted, in fact—was something more than what existed in the bedroom. What she wanted was someone more like herself. That was at the same time she had heard that Bryan had moved to Washington, accepting a position to teach at a college in suburban Maryland.

o

Mr. Pearson was burning the piles of leaves in the back yard, and from the kitchen window Katie watched the smoke rise and swirl into the murky drizzle.

"He's not much of a talker either," Donna said when she joined Katie in the kitchen. Donna had hooked Bryan up to a respirator which was kept in the house for Chris, and Bryan had quickly fallen asleep.

Everyone has a horror story, Katie thought. Mr. Pearson's wife had died of cancer last year. Donna's sister had contracted the virus from a blood transfusion she needed during an appendectomy.

When Donna's sister died, Donna began training as a home care-taker. "None of those doctors understand any of this," she told Katie. "What's worse, they have no compassion."

The worst thing that had happened to Chris was that he had discovered a lesion behind his left ear which a doctor had diagnosed as Kaposi's sarcoma. Chris began chemotherapy and then lost his job. He went on disability for a while, then moved to Washington and lived with a friend who was also ill. The friend was evicted, and Chris had landed in the hospital. When he was released he decided to live with his father in Virginia. Katie had learned Chris was in Virginia only last week, when she had taken a break from seeing Bryan in the hospital to help with a mailing for contributions for the meal service. She overheard a co-worker mention that Chris Pearson had moved. Katie and Bryan had lost track of Chris in the last year and a half, had not realized he was back in Washington; they had been absorbed too deeply in their own crisis. Or was there a deeper, more profound reason—that maybe Bryan and Chris were both too proud and too ashamed to admit to one another that they had fallen ill? There were times when Katie thought about trying to find Chris, but something prevented it, held her back. She knew it was her fear. If Bryan was sick—calm, rational Bryan—wouldn't that mean breezy, impulsive Chris might be, too? Or worse—perhaps he was already dead? Now Katie felt the worst thing that could have happened was that each might not have even known the other was sick. Or even worse, the absolute worst—she might not ever have been able to bring them back together again.

"You look fab-u-lous," Chris punctuated the syllables when he was awake and Katie sat on the edge of his chair. But before she could feel self-conscious, Chris turned his head toward Bryan and said, "But her, *what happened to her?*"

What had happened was that Bryan's T cells began to drop; he developed thrush first, then began a PCP prophylaxis, TMP/SMX. He developed mild allergic reactions and was switched to dapsone when it was discovered he had already developed toxoplasmosis, a parasite that infects the brain. When he began to have seizures, the dapsone was stopped and he developed pneumonia. But Katie told Chris none of this. Instead, she ran her fingers lightly across his arm and said, "Just some bad luck."

"Bad luck?" Chris smirked and Katie watched him chew the words around in his mind. "Is that the worst, *the absolute worst?*"

o

What is the worst that can happen? *The absolute worst?* A game played many times over the years. It had started during their trip through Europe. While driving through the countryside, they began playing silly games to pass the time—first I Spy, then License Plate. Later they began creating their own games; their favorite became Parents and Child. The two riding in the front seat were the Parents, the one in the back became the Child. It was the purpose of the Child to ask simple questions of the Parents, whose object was to reply in the most ridiculous manner possible. For example, the Child could ask, "How tall is the mountain? How wide is the river?" And the Parents would reply, "That mountain is taller than 150 seven-foot-tall men standing on top of each other." Or, "That river is wider than two hundred floating pregnant women." Katie always enjoyed playing Child more than Parent; she would sit forever in the back seat, asking endlessly annoying questions.

Then one day, a day that had begun with a frustrating sequence of events—a flat tire, no gas station, not enough of the right currency—Parents and Child evolved into What Is the Worst That Can Happen? The "worst" was not intended to alarm the players;

instead, it was created to inspire them with a sort of cynical hope: thinking of the absolute worst thing that could happen (for instance, the car could have been totaled and they could be broke) made what had happened (a flat tire and nothing but change) seem not that bad at all. Over the years, as they met again, spoke on the phone, and complained about jobs and lovers and money and weight, conversations began to end and begin with the question, "But is that the worst, *the absolute worst?*"

o

Chris did not stay awake for long, and Katie and Donna sat in the kitchen, clutching coffee mugs. Mr. Pearson came inside, smelling of wet, smoking leaves. Katie had not seen him in over thirteen years, since her college graduation, but she was aware as they greeted one another that their misfortunes were erasing the awkwardness of time.

"Did you know Hal?" Mr. Pearson asked, washing his hands at the sink.

"Hal?" Katie answered. "No. I don't think so."

"Someone called last night and said he had died. I didn't tell him yet."

"Now, now," Donna interrupted. "We don't need to tell him nothing. We just want to keep him comfortable."

Comfortable? Katie thought. In a house in the suburbs, a world so far removed from the one Chris had made his own? "I can tell him when he wakes up again," Katie said.

"No, that's all right," Mr. Pearson answered, and looked at Donna. "I guess we shouldn't make him feel any worse."

Katie noticed something pass between Donna and Mr. Pearson. What she saw was Mr. Pearson looking at Donna, Donna averting her eyes, smoothing her hair, a light tremble in her fingertips. She saw Mr. Pearson shuffling his feet, looking first at the floor, then out the window. It occurred to Katie that what was passing between them stretched beyond the boundaries of compassion. This was new love, she realized, testing and groping and tempting. Out of all this mess, life has to go on, she thought. She stood and said, "I'll go check on Bryan," leaving them alone, willing them to continue their looks and tension and sparks.

She sat beside Bryan, feeling foolish again. She turned and watched Chris sleeping, then looked again at Bryan, his closed eyelids fluttering as though he were dreaming. And then it occurred to Katie that there must have been a reason she had brought them back together. Was it because they had loved each other? Was it because she still loved them? Or was it because she had never expressed her love for them in the simple, passionate way she had once witnessed them share with each other?

And then what Katie remembered was the Alpine moonlight, the low soft moans, the shadows against a wall. What had happened was they had found a hostel outside of Innsbruck and had taken a room that had two double beds. Katie, tired from the drive and the mountain air, had fallen asleep quickly. Bryan and Chris had stayed awake, talking and planning the next day's trip. Sometime in the middle of the night Katie awoke with a chill. As she turned over and curled tighter into the blanket she heard the other bed creak. When she opened her eyes she noticed, from the splinters of moonlight which leaked into the room, Chris's head rising and falling over Bryan's body. She heard their heavy breathing, then noticed Bryan lifting, turning himself so that he was now on top of Chris, and she quietly drew them in closer, willed her eyes to drink in more light. What she saw was one of the most breathtaking experiences of her life, as moving and majestic as the European scenery. It was Bryan making love to Chris, Chris making love to Bryan, their arms and legs and bodies rising and falling in the chilly blue light.

She had re-created that night in her mind for years, had even tried to recapture the sensation of it with Ellen. It had always bothered Katie that she and Ellen had never achieved the type of easy relationship Bryan and Chris had. But it had always bothered her, too, that Bryan and Chris had lost touch with one another. Had something that had meant so much to her to observe meant so little to Bryan and Chris? Had they forgotten what they had felt for one another, or had Katie just imagined it, bit by bit by bit? Or did people just grow apart, move away from one another without looking back, without *wanting* to look back, as she and Ellen had done?

And then Katie felt discouraged, defeated. The visit had not gone as she had imagined. Bryan and Chris had not even been awake at the same time. What Katie had hoped for, had hoped to resurrect between Bryan and Chris, had not occurred. She began to worry that perhaps the trip had done more damage than good. Bryan seemed to have gotten worse since they arrived at the house. And she had only shown Chris that Bryan was also sick. What was worse, she might have destroyed, in her own mind, the passion of Bryan and Chris's relationship. After all these years, had she merely imagined it?

And now she had the worry of the drive back; she checked her watch and realized she was running late. How many doctors would yell at her? Would the hospital blame her if Bryan's condition worsened?

She found her purse and her coat and went into the kitchen to say goodbye. Mr. Pearson had retreated back outside, and Donna was preparing an IV solution she would later give to Chris.

"I'll help you get him back out to the car," Donna said.

While Donna was unhooking the respirator from Bryan, Bryan stirred into consciousness. He gave Donna a wide-eyed look, like a child who has just emerged from underwater. He looked around the room slowly, taking in Katie in her coat, the silent TV, the dark heavy paneling, then Chris, sleeping beside him. He lifted his hand a few inches into the air and placed it against a crease of Chris's robe; then his eyes searched through the air till they locked with Katie's. "No," Bryan said, in a rasp that cut through the silence of the room. "Not yet."

o

Later, as she was driving Bryan back to the hospital, traffic snarled where the highway ramp swept over the Potomac. Katie adjusted the mirror and looked at Bryan in the back seat, noticing he was awake, looking out at the view of the river and the buildings and the monuments. Now she imagined them playing another round of Parents and Child, but the questions kept twisting, darkening in her mind. Why did this happen? How many people will become infected? What will one learn from the great plague of AIDS? What is the worst, *the absolute worst,* that can happen?

Two friends will die, leaving one to tell their story. That is the worst, the absolute worst, that can happen.

WHO THE BOYS ARE

THE DREAM BEGINS AT THE BEACH. I AM LYING ON A TOWEL, MY face toward the sun. It is hot. I am sweating. Near me, my friends Jeff and Ricky are throwing a Frisbee to one another, though they have never met. My dog, Zero, dead since my childhood, chases the waves. The water breaks in white curls, sounding suspiciously like bubbles in an aquarium. The sky, at first blue, is suddenly filled with gray clouds that swirl together like a hurricane. There is a flash of light and I open my eyes. The dream is over. The light above my bed is on. I can feel the white cotton gown sticking to my skin. The respirator above the bed gurgles. My father sits at the foot of the bed in a chair, reading a magazine. He notices I am awake. "Some boys were here to see you," he says. "They said they'd be back. Went to get something to eat." I close my eyes and fall asleep again.

o

I am awake when Stuart and Vince enter the room. Though I have not been outside in what seems to be months, I know it must be raining. Stuart is wearing a tan raincoat. Vince carries a folding umbrella. They both lean over the bed, one at a time, and kiss me lightly on the cheek, saying "Hello," "How are you?" The chairs scrape across the floor as they are rearranged so Stuart and Vince can sit next to the bed. Stuart places his hand on top of mine.

I don't listen at first. I just stare. Their dark hair, brown eyes, lean bodies the same height, so similar they appear to be brothers. But different: Stuart's complexion lighter, his forehead broader; Vince's stubble of unshaven beard, hair peeking above the collar of his sweater. Stuart slumps forward in the chair as he talks. When I listen he is describing the house they are buying in Pennsylvania, built in the nineteenth century and once the general store for a town with a population not much larger than this room's. "The house is huge," he says. "Four bedrooms, two fireplaces, an attic, a cellar, a separate garage, which we think we might turn into a studio or guest cottage." Vince, usually the quietest of us when we are together, today fills the awkward pauses politely, offering explanations directed to my father: "Near Scranton," "Three and a half hours," "Weekends."

Sometimes I worry Vince thinks I hate him. We started off awkward. I, confused, jealous, that Stuart had a lover. He, confused, jealous, that I knew Stuart better than he. I have known Stuart since college, freshman year, when we met while taking art history. We shared an apartment off-campus for two years, discovered each other's preference for men during late-night study breaks, explored the bars downtown, teased one another about the young men we brought home, and spent a summer together in London. We moved to Manhattan, where we lived in an apartment in the

West Village: he to attend graduate school, I to start a job, each of us a friend to the other, each looking to find a lover.

My father tells Vince about a system which purifies well water. My father was always repairing, rebuilding our house outside Atlanta. Two years ago, he sold the house, and now lives in Florida.

A nurse enters and the chairs scrape across the floor again. She takes my temperature, pulse, and blood pressure and writes on the chart. I don't like this nurse, Thelma; she never has anything nice to say. Today she says, "Nothing new," before she leaves. I look down at my left arm, where she has left it on the bed. I hardly recognize it. The dark hair has turned light, the skin is blotched red and gray, there are circles of blue bruises bigger than the lesions on my thigh. If I even think about moving my arm it hurts; I am amazed that something so thin can feel so heavy, almost as heavy as the white gown which presses so hard against my chest I think it must be trying to stop my breath. Suddenly I want nothing more than to go back to sleep.

○

Alec brings flowers and messages from work: Reyna, our secretary, picked out the tulips, Don says hello and plans to visit, Frank, the security guard, is getting married in the summer, and Martin, our boss, wants to know what I think about a Friday-night horror series. Each comment is expelled rapidly in his thin, breathless voice before his coat is off. Though I remember telling everyone to stop bringing me things, Alec always arrives with something. He pulls an enamel pin, shaped and painted in the design of a 1950s television set, from his coat pocket, flashes it in front of me like his smile, and pins it to my gown.

He looks so healthy and winsome, dressed in a blue shirt, a red sweater vest, and gray pleated pants. He introduces himself to my father and shakes his hand firmly. His smooth, round face, and light freckles make him look so innocent and boyish. For years he tried to look older, so people would take him seriously. He grew a mustache that made his upper lip seem too wide, and then a beard that sprouted only in patches. He tried wearing dark, tailored clothes to look more professional, and thick black plastic eyeglasses to look studious. Now they are gone and the contacts he wears brighten the color of his amber eyes. Now he looks comfortable, relaxed, youthful. At the television network where we work everyone, after seven years, is aware his intelligence and opinions are invaluable. He can zip off how many episodes of an old TV series were shot, naming the directors, stars, and supporting cast without checking the reference files; he can read the script of a series pilot and tell why it won't work but how it can be made better. Once he saved my neck when he vetoed a suggestion for a comedy special televised live from a nightclub; though I thought it would work, he remembered another network had tried it and failed.

When I was admitted this time I refused to allow anyone to turn on the TV beside the bed. I didn't want to be reminded that I was missing work. And I didn't need the distraction; my roommate, a young man with a hacking cough, kept his set on all day, all night, the sound spilling above, below, and around the heavy plastic partition which separated us. I was relieved when he left and the doctor decided to keep his bed empty.

Alec sits on the edge of the bed and slips an arm beneath my body. Swiftly, deftly, he lifts my head and shoulders and flips over my pillows, something he knows makes me happy, since I asked him to do it the last time I was in the hospital.

I have always had a crush on Alec. Thanksgiving, the first year we met, we were walking together down Seventh Avenue after dinner. Alec had just broken up with his first lover and moved into an apartment in Chelsea. The sidewalk was slick from a rain which had just stopped, and everything about the city seemed suspended, briefly, in order to catch a breath. But Alec went on and on, his voice nasal from a cold, about what a rat his old boyfriend was. As we turned down his block, I caught the smell of wet pine from the trees roped together and leaning against the wall of a building, waiting to be sold for Christmas. It made me feel so special and yet lonely. His apartment, a railroad flat, was decorated as mine had been in those days: cardboard boxes disguised with sheets, painted wood fruit crates, and threadbare chairs. We sat on his sofa drinking martinis, a new taste we had both acquired, and as I was trying to comfort him about his lover, we started to kiss. We rolled off the sofa, landed on the floor with a thump, and laughed.

"Are we this crazy?" he asked.

"Desperate, you mean," I replied.

"It'll be OK," he says now, while straightening the sheets of the bed, just as he had reassured me of my job when I was troubled by insecurities, just as I had remarked when he was disappointed about his broken relationship.

A doctor enters the room. My father stands up from his chair and the doctor places his hand on my father's shoulder. Alec leads my father out of the room. The doctor doesn't even read my chart. He presses his hands against my neck, underneath my arms, around my wrists, as though examining for broken bones. I don't like this doctor. I don't even know his name. He tells me he wants to take more blood. What can I do? More tests, more results, never any answers.

o

Another dream: I am swimming in the dark. A pool or maybe a lake. The water is thick and heavy but it feels good to be moving.

My breathing is short and troubled but when I dive underneath and hold my breath it feels like I'm flying.

A white line separates the darkness. As it brightens I see a road speeding beneath me, a tunnel of trees on either side. When the road disappears I continue flying: over a lake, a field of wild flowers, then another road, and then a mountain. I stop when I reach a crowd of faces. The only one I recognize is my mother. As I touch her white hair it is bright again.

Awake, I am hungry, as though all my exercise, my dreaming, has created an appetite. I haven't had any real food in weeks. Nutrition, a clear liquid, is pumped from a plastic bag through a tube connected to my vein.

My father stares at the view from the window, twelve floors above the East River. I have never seen this view; the blinds were closed when I arrived, and from where I lie I can only imagine what he sees: the slow barges on the water, the glint of light on cars crossing the bridge, and the hollow windows of the subway train floating beneath, planes bisecting the horizon, a tipsy helicopter paused beside a building like a hummingbird before a flower. A view of motion, paths crossing, nothing connecting; if it does, it's an accident or a disaster. I wish I could tell my father about my dream, that I saw my mother, but there is a raspy scratch at the back of my throat reminding me I cannot speak.

o

Jeff is here. He is late, he says, because he ran into my super and explained the faucet in the bathroom needed fixing. Jeff is the one who has taken care of me these last few months, though he was my best friend long before I got sick. He takes me to doctors, cleans my apartment, checks my messages and mail, and waters the plants, so I don't have to worry. I worry anyway. I worry about the bills and the insurance and that this feeling of helplessness will never end. Last month, when I didn't have enough to pay the rent, Jeff called a list of my friends and asked each for fifty dollars to contribute toward the rent. Now I worry he will leave me, decide he's had enough of all this. The first time I was in the hospital he was always asking about my food and medicine. Had I eaten? Did I want anything special? What pill is that? How often do I need it? Once he yelled at me when a nurse brought me medication and when she left the room I dumped it into the trash. "It hurts my stomach," I said. "But maybe there's something else you can try," he answered.

Jeff is the one who decorated my hospital room with tinsel and a tiny artificial Christmas tree, the green branches covered with silver ornaments and pale-blue lights. He taped the Christmas cards to the wall and arranged a small party for me on Christmas Eve with presents and friends. Jeff is also the one who called my father. On Christmas Day, which I don't even remember, he told my father I was sick. He explained everything to him, as he told me later, in a calm but precise manner. The next day my father was here, at the hospital, and I know Jeff was relieved not to have to make that other call, the one which would have included, "Oh, you didn't know?"

Jeff brings the chair close to the bed and spreads the mail, which he has pulled from a plastic bag, across the white sheet. He holds each piece in front of me and says, "Bill," "Letter," or "Garbage," and sorts them into piles. He does this, I know, to show me my life still goes on, though I have given him the power to end it if it gets any worse. He reads me the letters out loud. Today there are two and a postcard. The postcard, a photo of giant ruby slippers beneath a palm tree, is from Clark, a friend who works at the video store on my block, who went to Hawaii for a vacation. One letter is actually a late Christmas card from

Jackson, the mail boy at work, saying he is thinking of me. The other is from Ricky, and as Jeff reads it I notice my father lean forward in his chair. My father always liked Ricky. In the summers he used to take us to the Okefenokee to canoe and spot alligators, something Ricky still does. I want to tell Jeff to stop reading, I already know about Ricky's life: his blond wife, his two kids, his job as an economist for a bank. When he finishes reading it he hands it to my father, and then scoops up the mail and returns it to the plastic bag.

Jeff is the one I will miss most. I think this is hardest on him: my life interrupting his. He met my father at the airport, won't let him lift a finger while he stays at my apartment, takes him out to dinner. Before my father arrived Jeff told me he took the magazines and videos I had on the top shelf of my closet over to his apartment. I feel so dishonest; I've nothing to give him, not even a voice to say thanks.

Jeff has always reminded me of summer, of chlorinated water, of white beaches and beautiful boys. In a way, he is an extension of the Ricky I knew as a kid, perhaps the reason I was first attracted to him. Unclothed, he has a swimmer's body. We met doing laps in the pool at the Y. His handsomeness immediately awed me: with his broad shoulders, thin waist, high cheekbones, and square jaw, stepping like someone I admired in a book or a magazine off the page and into my life. He works as a catalogue designer, and though he can afford to dress like the high-paid models he selects for photographs, he is usually simply dressed in a plain-colored shirt, old jeans, and sneakers.

Now I can hear Jeff running the water at the sink. Soon he is washing me with a warm cloth. He is not afraid to touch me, like some of the nurses. My father watches Jeff's every stroke; I'm surprised he's not embarrassed at the affection between two boys.

Though I can't smell my filth, my stench, because of the respirator, I can feel it on every pore of my body. My hair is matted; I want to shower, shave. But the cloth feels nice, and Jeff quickly dries me with a clean towel after he has washed a portion of my skin, afraid I will become chilled. When he finishes he combs my hair lightly with the brush I keep in the drawer beside the bed.

"Better?" he says, and though I cannot answer, I know he is, too. All this action, movement, is calming for him. If he stopped for a moment he would become depressed, worried, scared. I know him. Now he begins to convince my father he should get something to eat. My father looks at me and then at Jeff, but Jeff is already at the door, waiting. "Rest," Jeff says to me, and then, to my father, "He can use the rest. You can use the food."

o

It must be hot in the room. Trey removed his jacket after only a few minutes, then his tie, then unbuttoned his shirt and rolled up the sleeves. The first time he visited me I could see the anxiety etched across his face: he was worried he could end up in this room; the predictions say he might.

Shivering, I feel another fever taking hold. My body doesn't seem able to shake the pneumonia this time. It's odd to be so cold in a room so hot and dry. Trey does not talk; he simply takes my hand and entwines our fingers together. I can still see him the night we met at Alec's party. It was April, two years ago, and the windows were open, a breeze gently flipping the flames of a row of burning candles on a bookshelf. We were both holding drinks. There was something mysterious about him. Perhaps it was his dark, well-trimmed beard. Or the black eyes, or the flat eyebrows which ran into one another at the bridge of his nose. We talked so long our glasses left wet circles on the coffee table.

We were lovers after that first night. Every day I discovered something new about him: the grandson of Rumanian immigrants, a stint teaching English in Portugal, a passion for cinnamon pancakes. When he left I wasn't surprised; after a year together he was still a mystery to me. He was so private and secretive I had not met any of his friends. He said I monopolized the relationship: we ate at restaurants I chose, went to movies I wanted to see, stayed at my apartment instead of his. I was inflexible and he was a puzzle.

The night I was diagnosed I called and left a message on his answering machine. "Murderer," I said, and hung up. I don't know why I did it; I don't blame him. There were others. Maybe I wanted to jolt something so the pieces would fall together. Maybe I wanted to hurt him the way he had hurt me when he left.

Now Trey's eyes are glassy. Any minute I think he may cry. But he seems fine when my father and Jeff walk into the room. Jeff and Trey hug one another, and then Jeff introduces Trey to my father. They shake hands and there is an awkward, silent pause. If I could talk I would yell at them, "Go home. There's nothing else you can do."

o

My father reads a magazine, stares out the window, watches and listens to the boys come and go. Minutes go by that are as long as days. The days pass, blurring into one another. I know he must be full of questions: How did this happen? Why to my son? Such fine-looking young men, why aren't they married?

My mother said I had his looks at an early age: his wavy hair, the dimple in his chin, his wide brow, his straight lips, his hazel eyes, his aquiline nose. I know my father must be shocked to see his son, barely thirty, looking older than himself. My sunken eyes, my mottled skin, what hair I have left from chemotherapy now white.

His parents, my grandparents, are dead. My mother died of cancer three years ago. He had only one son, only one child. All the blood he has left lies in this bed. I want to tell him so much before I fall asleep again, before the dreams do not disappear. I love you and please don't hate me. . . . I love you and please understand that I didn't tell you because I thought you might be angry or disappointed in me. . . . I love you and I don't want to die. . . . I love you and I always wanted to explain my life but I was afraid it would hurt you. . . . I love you and I want to tell you who these boys are. A moment before sleep I feel sure he must understand. I am his only son, his only child. I am him. And these boys are me. . . .

JADE

THE PLANE DROPPED THROUGH A POCKET OF AIR LIKE A KITE IN
search of wind. Mae, unnerved, looked up from her compact mirror
in the direction of the stewardess, but the perky young woman
showed no sign of alarm. The plane dropped again and Mae cursed
under her breath. The stewardess walked down the aisle, smiling,
whispering, "Please fasten your seat belts. The plane is landing."

Every winter Mae flew nonstop to Florida. Since her grandson
Seth's funeral, however, Mae had decided a stopover was necessary
this year. Seth's illness had revealed a shroud her grandson kept
over his life from his family. All at once Mae had learned in a
phone call that Seth was in the hospital, dying, and his lover, Ty,
was already dead. A year ago Mae had not even known her grandson
was gay.

Mae let the cabin empty before she moved from her seat. She
stood and discreetly adjusted her bra beneath the sleeveless knit

137

blouse she wore, then buttoned the old cream-colored sweater at the neck, draping it across her shoulders like a cape. The stewardess approached and handed Mae the cane that had been stored in an overhead compartment. Mae ran her palm over the polished crook of the cane, then lifted her purse and shopping bag from the floor.

"Someone should say something to your friend that maybe he should go back for some flying lessons. No wind. No storm. And still they try to terrorize old women into heart attacks while landing a plane."

"I'm sorry, ma'am," the stewardess said. "We hit some minor turbulence. Nothing serious. I hope the rest of your flight was peaceful."

"Peaceful?" Mae asked, shocked at the girl's use of the word. "What's so peaceful about the lady next to me jumping up every time a man without a wedding band headed in the direction of the restroom?"

Mae stopped herself. She was doing it again. That cranky, whining old-woman routine. "I'm sorry, dear," she said to the stewardess. "Still crabby from the nap." Mae laughed deeply, from the bottom of her chest, till it leapt into a girlish cackle.

The stewardess smiled, then said mechanically, "Hope you enjoyed the flight. Bye-bye."

When the ramp descended into the terminal, Mae recognized Ty's daughter, Janna, from the photo she had seen in Seth's apartment. Janna was a handsome, thirtyish black woman, big-boned, with skin the color of milk chocolate. Mae knew instantly it was going to be a tough meeting from the frown on Janna's face.

Mae approached and introduced herself. "Mae Steinberg," she said.

Janna forced a smile; her lips tightened over the expanse of teeth. "I'm Janna," she said. "How was your flight?"

"That pilot, such a *shmendrik*." Mae rolled her eyes. "Couldn't fly a toy airplane. And every time I dozed off one of those *farkakte* girls was hovering over me with a drink. Can't they let you be? Why do they all think they have to entertain like MGM?" Mae caught herself again with a deep breath and changed gears. "You're so pretty. Just like I imagined. And such lovely green eyes."

Janna forced another smile.

Actually Mae had been unprepared for Janna's beauty; was startled, in fact, by the striking angles of her face and the vivid color of her eyes. Mae tried to remember if Seth had ever talked of Janna, but nothing about her came immediately to mind.

"Such a lovely dress you're wearing," Mae said.

"Would you like to get a bite to eat?" Janna asked.

Mae noticed the woman's tone was cold and businesslike.

"Oh, no. Just a drink," Mae said.

"There's a place just at the corner there." Janna pointed.

Mae waved her cane in the air and smiled. "It's more for effect," she said. "It's so everyone will know I'm a crotchety old woman."

"Oh, I'm sure that's not so." Janna laughed, revealing at last a nice, normal smile.

"But it is," Mae said. "I *am* a cranky old woman. I *like* being a cranky old woman. Sometimes," she added, and winked at Janna.

Janna headed toward a table in the back, away from the concourse, but Mae stopped her by tugging on her sleeve. "Dear, let's sit at the bar," she said. "Be daring."

They took seats at the lip of the bar. Mae lifted herself to perch on a stool.

"There's never any air in these places," Mae said. "*Mechaieh*. Just that fake chill." Mae could feel herself breathing heavily. She wondered if it was from their brisk walk to the bar, her nervousness, or perhaps, even, simply from her old age.

A waitress approached the two women and placed napkins in front of them.

"I'll have a ginger ale," Janna said.

"Ginger ale?" Mae asked, alarmed. "What do you have? An ulcer?"

"No, no. Nothing like that. Just a sour stomach," Janna explained.

Just the stomach? Mae thought to herself, then wondered if her presence made Janna miserable, a recognition of her father's other life or a reminder of his absence. Mae flipped her hand in the air to attract the waitress. "Beer," Mae said. "Something low-cal."

The waitress turned and disappeared. Janna's attention was diverted to the opposite end of the concourse, where a row of servicemen in khaki uniforms leaned in various positions against the wall.

"They look so relaxed," Janna said. "Just like everyone else. But they're all dressed up like toys."

"Toys?" Mae wondered out loud and stared at the servicemen. "Really? Do they belong to us?"

"What?" Janna asked.

"American?" Mae asked.

"Yes," Janna answered. "There's a base just south of the city."

The waitress returned with their drinks and set them on the napkins. She took a sponge and began wiping the bar next to Janna. Mae stared at a mirror hanging over the bar, above the waitress's head. "What have they written on it?" she asked Janna, and pointed into the air, the bracelets on her wrist falling down her arm with a series of tiny clinks and clanks. "There."

Janna looked up at the mirror. "It's a type of peach liqueur."

"Really?" Mae glanced at the mirror again, trying to focus the words, then called to the waitress, "Miss! Miss!" The waitress put her sponge down.

"Could I try one of those?" Mae pointed to the sky, her bracelets again clanking and clinking.

The waitress looked up, then at Mae. "Straight up?"

"What?" Mae asked.

"Straight or on the rocks?" the waitress asked again.

"A little ice would be nice, thank you," Mae answered.

The waitress disappeared and returned with a small glass filled with a golden liquid. She placed it in front of Mae. Mae thought the shivers of ice in the glass made the drink seem to sparkle.

"Bitter," Mae said, pursing her lips, when she had tasted the liqueur. "Want a taste?" she asked Janna.

"No, thanks," Janna answered.

"Let me show you my great-grandson," Mae said, and reached for her purse. She pulled her eyeglasses from the chain on her neck and placed them on her face. From her purse she pulled out a yellow envelope twisted with rubber bands. She unraveled the envelope and began showing pictures to Janna.

"That's my daughter, Judy, and her husband, Mitchell, in front of their house in Fairfield. Seth's parents," she said. "And that's Seth's brother, Nate, and his wife when I went out to their house on Long Island. Here we go. That's Josh. Eight days old. Just before the bris. Isn't he perfect?"

"He's beautiful," Janna said, leaning into Mae.

"Children are always beautiful," Mae said. "No matter how old they get to be."

Mae wrapped the photographs back up in the envelope. "And you? Don't you have a little girl?" Mae asked.

Janna, looking embarrassed at the sudden switch of attention toward herself, answered, "Yes. Daycee. She's four now."

"Such a wonderful age, you know. They're so bright and still learning. Is she in kindergarten?"

"Preschool." Janna smiled. Mae thought that at last Janna seemed to be warming up.

"She must keep you busy."

"Oh, yes," Janna said with a heavy laugh. "Last night she wouldn't go to sleep until I read her 'The Princess and the Pea.' For the seventh time that day. And then she made me take her bed apart and show her there was nothing hidden under her mattress."

"She sounds so adorable," Mae said, smiling, fingering the gold chain at her neck. "And your husband? He's still a salesman for computers?"

Mae could tell by Janna's frown that she had gone too far, stepped over a line, remembered too much personal information.

"Yes, yes," Janna answered tensely. "He just got a new store. We thought he might be transferred, but we made it through all the cutbacks."

Mae looked up at the mirror above the bar, wondering if it was blurry because her eyesight was so bad or because of the drinks. She lifted her glasses to her eyes and squinted till everything came into focus.

"You didn't need to come all this way," Janna said.

"Come where?" Mae asked, and waved her hand. "I'm on my way to Miami. Too much time in the air and God might send me to heaven before I land. A stopover's good. A break in the journey."

Janna looked down at her drink, having nothing else to say.

"Besides, I thought we should meet. Your mother. My daughter. All those phone calls. And now, because Ty and Seth are both dead, they think nobody has to talk anymore. *Shanda.*" Mae could feel that cranky edge rising within her. She pulled herself back and continued. "And we found this when cleaning Seth's apartment. You should have it."

Mae handed Janna the small shopping bag. Janna reached her hand into the bag and pulled out a thick but little black leather-bound book. Janna rubbed the book with her hand, finding the crease of the cover where it had been bent over the edge of the pages for so many years.

"My father's Bible," Janna said. "I haven't seen this since . . ." Her voice trailed off.

Mae watched the astonishment erase the tension from Janna's expression as she pressed her hand against the cover of the Bible. Janna flipped through the pages, stopping at a page where her ancestors had recorded their births and weddings and deaths.

"So old." Mae lifted her head at Janna. "It must be worth a fortune."

Janna continued staring at the Bible.

"Your father. He was a real *mensch,*" Mae said.

"What?" Janna asked.

"Salt of the earth," Mae explained.

"You never met him, did you?" Janna said.

"What?"

"My father."

"No," Mae said. "He and Seth were very private. They kept it a secret from us. Till he died and then Seth told us."

Mae watched Janna for some sort of emotional response, but her face had returned to its austere, restrained composure.

"When he was in the hospital Seth told me some wonderful stories about him," Mae said. "Such a smart man. A good man. He must have been, to have loved my grandson."

"He never believed in God, you know," Janna said.

"What?" Mae asked. "God?" She felt suddenly abandoned, lost.

She caught her breath. "But he believed in so many other things," Mae said. "In freedom. In trust. In love. It was as if he *had* to believe in God."

Janna lifted her eyes to meet Mae's. She smiled thinly, hiding her teeth.

"I never meant to seem that I disapproved of them," Janna said. "You just don't think things like that about your father."

"Now, now, dear," Mae said. "I know he must have loved you very much." Mae took her hand and placed it on top of Janna's.

"Those are lovely bracelets," Janna said, touching the bracelets Mae wore on her wrist. Mae knew Janna was trying again to deflect the attention away from herself.

"Jade," Mae answered, and noticed they were the same color as Janna's eyes. "They belonged to my sister." By instinct Mae rubbed her other hand across the smooth stone surfaces and twisted her wrist in the air so that the bracelets slid down her arm, catching the overhead light.

Mae looked at the bracelets, then at Janna's eyes, noticing how oddly Janna's concentration focused, sharpened, and changed. Mae looked again at the bracelets and knew Janna had noticed not the color of the stones, nor the play of light, but instead the small list of numbers tattooed below Mae's wrist.

Janna looked away from Mae, at her drink, then at the mirror above the bar.

"I must find that gate now," Mae said. "Miss! Miss!" Mae yelled. "Can we have a check? Why do they always disappear just when you need them?"

The waitress returned and Mae paid for the check, over Janna's objections, and Janna walked Mae to a gate at the other end of the concourse.

"I met your grandson once in New York," Janna said as they

reached the gate. "I was about three months pregnant, and we had dinner together with my father. Seth didn't know I knew about him and my dad. I hated every minute of that dinner. I was so insulted that my father would put us at the same table. And then, when the check came, Seth and my dad started fighting over the bill. Seth insisted he pay for his dinner, but my father wouldn't let him. They didn't speak to each other the rest of the night."

Janna looked around at the assembling crowd of passengers, then back at Mae. "I was still so young then," she said, bowing her head toward the floor as if praying. "I didn't understand a lot of things. But I could tell by their silence that night that they cared very much for each other."

Mae, surprised by Janna's remembrance, watched Janna slowly move the hand that carried her father's Bible and place it against her breast.

"I'm sorry," Janna said, as the stewardess announced that Mae's flight was to begin boarding.

"You're sorry. I'm sorry." Mae shook her head. "These are personal sorries. Should Mr. President fall sick with this *mishegoss,* then the doctors will finally be sorry. That's what the world's come to."

"No. I mean—" Janna started, confused.

"I know," Mae said. "I know."

Mae felt self-conscious and displaced in the awkward silence that followed, till Janna leaned over and kissed her on the cheek.

"I'm glad I came to meet you," Janna said, walking with Mae toward the ramp.

"Me? A cranky old woman with too much jewelry?" Mae answered, and shrugged her shoulders. "I must thank *you,*" she said, "for letting me know my grandson was happy."

Janna frowned again but thawed as Mae patted her on the

shoulder and said goodbye. Mae turned and headed up the ramp, rattling her bracelets in the air with a wave before she disappeared out of Janna's sight.

Once again in the air, Mae complained to the stewardess about the food and the pillow and the crying baby behind her. Before the plane landed, the pilot veered the plane into a wide arc. Below, Mae studied the Florida coast. What a lovely shade of green, she thought, noticing the color of the sea where it turned shallow just before land.

GHOSTS

WHEN I FIRST MET SCOTT, HE WAS WAITING TO SEE THE DOCTOR, waiting to be injected with ribavirin.

"The first week was awful," he told me that day. "I was getting worse. I was constantly coughing and running a fever. Then I started getting better. I've really stabilized."

I am not surprised that now, almost a year later, as I sit on the deck of a boat which is harbored by the pier, I can recall the images so vividly from that day. Scott was seated in the stark white waiting room, dressed in faded jeans and a faded red T-shirt which approached the color pink, and the dark-black letters that had once vividly spelled PARADISE across his chest had cracked and dissolved into gray. His body, which was trim and well defined, leaned in my direction, and he spoke in a voice I found remarkably calm. I did not imagine him sick; his complexion was exceptionally clear and showed no sign of illness or even aging. He had a face somewhere between handsome and pretty, with soft green eyes and a thin, long-lipped mouth that had broken into an alluring smile when he spoke his name. It was a face I felt belonged in a magazine, with a slender, unmarked nose, a solid, square-cut chin, and sandy-brown hair which was long and straight except where it had been cropped razor-short at the sides, and which shimmered blond when he tilted his head back into the light. But it was his winsome manner that made him seem so relaxed, levelheaded, not pointed toward panic. What I am surprised at now is that I can recall with equal clarity the emotions which pulled me toward Scott, feelings that stretched beyond any motivation of desire. It was the thought that here we were, two young, metropolitan males, suddenly rendered helpless by the science of our bodies. And it was this helplessness that introduced us to each other and kept us talking while we waited for answers.

"I'm not on a research program," Scott had said. "I had to go to Mexico to get it," he added, and began to explain his trip. I listened to him tell the story of a Mexican pharmacist who had agreed to sell him a larger quantity of the drug than was permitted, and how he had smuggled the excess across the border in an empty shampoo bottle.

I cannot remember what amazed me more, the fact that we had begun talking so easily and quickly, as though we were old friends, or my realization that even though Scott was sick from a virus that terrified me, I still felt an attraction to him. But I do remember I was astonished, even elated, that in spite of the aura cast by this disease, the power of attraction to another man had not diminished.

"I can't begin to tell you how many doctors I have now or have had, in all meanings of the phrase," Scott said, his eyes brightening. "And you?"

"I hope it's just an allergy," I said, and noticed Scott did not react to my expectation that I was healthy. I explained I was here at the insistence of my lover, Ben, who three weeks ago had adopted a puppy, a collie which he had named Batello. I told him I had been allergic to dogs for many years, since the death of my first dog, a cocker spaniel I had named Pensacola because I had wanted to be anywhere except the hot rural town in the middle of Alabama which my parents called my home. I told Scott that Cola, as I came to call her, had been my companion for twelve years and had stayed at my side as I grew into my teens, and that when she died I had become so distraught my parents had gotten another dog immediately, which I rejected just as quickly by developing a rash. Last week Ben had seen the doctor about an allergy. Two days ago I started itching and a rash had started beneath my arm. I told Scott I was here because Ben wanted me to have a checkup and get a prescription so we would not have to give Batello away. "He's grown so attached to him," I said to Scott. "He even sleeps in bed with us."

When the nurse called his name, Scott stood and offered his hand. I shook it and said I was glad we had met and, since I had not lived in the city for long, it was nice to find someone friendly. Scott said he was listed in the phone book, if I ever wanted to call, and we stood in front of each other, smiling awkwardly. Before he turned to leave I said that I hoped we might run into each other again, that I did not have many friends outside of the ones my lover knew.

"Hope," he replied before disappearing through the door. "It's such a wonderful word."

Now, looking back on the events of that day, I realize something extraordinary happened that afternoon in the waiting room. For a moment, only a very brief moment, I had been suspended in the space between sex and death.

o

"Remove your clothes," the nurse said, pointing to a set of hooks and hangers, when I had followed her into the examination room. "And slip this on," she added, placing a white hospital gown onto the examination table and leaving the room.

Though the room was chilly and smelled strongly of antiseptic, I remember I wasn't anxious or worried as I waited for the doctor. But when the doctor entered the room I was shocked at how unpleasant he looked. He was an extremely overweight and balding young man, with dark, beady eyes and a tiny gold-stud earring in his left ear, not at all my image of how a doctor should appear.

I sat on top of the examination table and described, in a series of broken, breathless phrases, the rash which was beginning underneath my right arm. The doctor first checked my pulse and heartbeat, touching my arm and chest, I thought, a bit too suggestively, before slipping the gown off my shoulder and examining the rash.

He began to ask me a series of questions: "Are you diabetic? Are you constipated? Have you had a lot of headaches or fevers recently? Have you been under a lot of stress?"—the last of which I answered with an uneasy "Yes," explaining I had just moved to San Francisco, had recently started a new job, gotten a new dog, and had just become involved in a relationship with Ben, who had recently seen the doctor.

"Ah yes, Ben," the doctor said, and wrote furiously on a notepad. I was alarmed at the tone of his voice and I flushed, feeling embarrassed as an eruption of sweat began across my forehead.

He took my temperature and began feeling the glands in my neck, armpits, and groin.

I remember thinking as he continued touching me that something awful was happening, that something was seriously wrong. I remember the future shriveling up, disappearing instantly from my vision; everything I had ever planned or wanted to do, to learn, to see suddenly seemed not possible. I wouldn't be able to meet Ben's friends for dinner this weekend. I wouldn't make it to the symphony tomorrow night. And then what worried me most was, I might not even make it home to see Ben again. I was sure an ambulance was already on its way to whisk me to the hospital. Panicking, I began to breathe rapidly.

"I'm going to give you a prescription for an ointment," the doctor said, returning to his notepad. "Rub it on once a day, after showering, and have this other prescription filled. Take the tablets three times a day, as directed."

"It's just a rash?" I asked, somewhat confused.

"Just a rash. Probably an allergic reaction. It could be from a new type of soap you've used, deodorant, detergent, maybe clothing or some sort of food. Maybe the dog. And it may be aggravated by stress, a new environment, changes in temperature. Allergy tests are complicated and expensive. Sometimes the problem clears of itself. Stay away from dairy products for a week, and be sure to drink plenty of water. If it's not better in two weeks, call for another appointment."

I felt momentarily relieved, until the doctor cleared his throat, slumped his shoulders forward, and started talking again.

"I'm advising all of my patients to have blood tests done. The results would remain anonymous and confidential."

I knew immediately what he was suggesting. I stared at the doctor in horror.

"It's not mandatory," he said. "It's your decision."

"Do you mean I have it?" The words choked at the back of my throat.

"No, no. Not at all. Only that you're in a high-risk category. And whatever the result, we can establish a base for monitoring any changes. Think it over for a few minutes. I'll get the nurse to bring you some pamphlets describing the test. Read them, and I'll be back in a few minutes."

As I watched him leave the room I felt a startled anger rise within me. Did the doctor think I was ignorant? I knew the statistics. I knew the number infected was staggering. I had friends who had died, others who were sick. Only a few minutes earlier I had talked about this very thing in this doctor's waiting room with Scott. And then it seemed as if every man I had ever known was sitting beside me in this room, worried, suspicious, and scared. I knew I wasn't ready to take this test. I was scared of the result. And what of Ben? I felt this was something I needed, *wanted,* to discuss with Ben first.

No, I decided, my heart hammering the ribs of my chest like a fist. Not now. Not yet. I needed some time to think. I jumped off the edge of the examination table and hurriedly dressed, shaking my head as I passed the nurse in the hall. On the sidewalk, I couldn't control the weakness in my legs, my body wavering as though I had just landed after a stormy cruise at sea. I sat down on the curb and bent my head between my legs, hoping to arrest the feeling of nausea, trying to calm myself by repeating the doctor's original diagnosis in my brain: "Just a rash, just a rash." But as I began to feel better I could not forget the terror the doctor had instilled, that something dangerous and uncontrollable could possibly be lurking unknown, hidden somewhere inside my body.

Even though I had known all along it was possible. I had known for years that who I was put me at risk.

o

It was Mark who first tried to set things right, put things in perspective. He was standing over the stove in the kitchen of his apartment, vigorously stirring the steaming vegetables in a wok.

"Therapy won't help you unless you tell yourself you're ready to be helped," he said.

I was seated at a small table for two in the corner of the kitchen, not listening to anything Mark was saying, just running my fingers across the plastic red-and-white-checked tablecloth and watching the hem of Mark's linen shirt float around his waist as he darted between the stove, the sink, and the cupboards. Maggie, Mark's rangy yellow cat, jumped up off the floor and into my lap and pawed at my thighs before deciding to rest.

"What you have to do is understand why it happened." Mark broke his concentration from the vegetables and looked at me. "Once you come to terms with that, you can move on to other points."

It had been four days since my visit to the doctor. But Mark was talking about my lover, Ben, who had been dead exactly four days. Mark and Ben had been best friends for sixteen years, but I had known Mark for only a little over six months. "He's re-formed," is the way Ben had described Mark before I ever met him, which meant that Mark had reacted to the possibility of becoming ill, as Ben explained, in a slightly obsessive way. Mark was an investment banker, and a rather handsome one at that, who had spent several years developing a striking physique. He had deep-brown eyes, a thick, dark mustache, and wavy black hair which not only covered the top of his head but was dispersed across his entire massive frame. He had a closet full of pin-striped suits and starched white shirts, but in the days before his reformation he had whirled through the streets of San Francisco in jeans, a flannel shirt, and a flight jacket. Now Mark remained at home, romping in his kitchen in linen shirts, learning macrobiotic cooking, and limiting his social life to a small circle of friends.

"Not in here you don't, baby," Mark had said, slapping Ben's hand, the first night I met Mark. We were at his apartment, squeezed three at the table for two, and Ben was about to light a cigarette. "I don't understand people who still smoke, drink, do drugs, or eat whatever they want," Mark had ranted. "They are only getting closer to death. They don't honestly cherish their lives."

"Listen to the Queen of the Quickies." Ben grinned. "Your kingdom used to be the trash heap, as I recall."

"It's true," Mark said, and turned to me. "I was driven by obsession. But if you recall, my dear Ben," and he turned to Ben, "I was always one who gorged, then purged."

"Stuff the cream puffs, then vomit." Ben laughed.

"Terrible." Mark rocked his head back and forth and smiled. "I was compelled."

"Mark once had five different men in one night," Ben remarked. "And each of them walked away satisfied."

"It was four, and a jerk behind the Troc," Mark corrected.

The night it was just the two of us, the cat, and the steaming vegetables, Mark defended his current preoccupation. "It's not just a diet. It's a way of looking at life. It's getting into tune with things."

"Now is hardly the time to be cleaning up your act," Ben had yelled a few weeks before at Mark, when he thought the obsessiveness was becoming, well, too obsessive.

"I should have been like this before," Mark said to me. "I only hope it doesn't catch up with me." Maggie the cat leapt from my lap and raced toward the window, curious about the sound of voices which drifted up from the sidewalk. Mark placed a bowl of bean soup on the table.

"I miss him," Mark confessed to me when he returned to the table with bowls of brown rice and vegetables. "I wish I knew why I'm doing so well. I'm going to be the last living clone."

o

I was not prepared for Ben's death. Often, as I think of him now, I am overcome by a weightless trance, a lightness of sensation, as if I have been lifted off the ground and suspended in midair. I think, perhaps, that has a lot to do with the way I remember Ben and I made love together. Ben's hands, long and slender, were always in constant motion. Our first nights in bed, as we explored and touched and studied one another, I remember his hands shifting and rolling and spinning our bodies together as though we were creating some sort of new, magical dance.

Ben had the capacity to make me feel as if I had been the only man who had ever existed in his life, or that anyone who came before me never really mattered or amounted to much. I remember how he would sleep beside me in bed, his head pressed against my neck, the moisture from his breath warming my skin. I remember the way his body would sometimes surprisingly envelop mine in the middle of the night. I remember how he would take his hand and cup my chin, tilt my head until my eyes met his, and then smile and draw us together into a kiss. Ben made me feel special and significant, in much more than just sexual ways. I remember how he would watch me in a crowded room, the way he would refer to me in a conversation, the ease with which he introduced me to his friends. I remember the way he would wait for me outside the building where I worked, the way his voice sounded as we walked home to our apartment. And I remember the nights when we would be visiting Mark, how Ben would slip his arm around my shoulders and listen to my opinions or my stories, even though he had heard them all a dozen times before.

Sometimes I feel it is hard to explain my connection to Ben. Though we were physically dissimilar—I was shorter, bulkier, fairer than Ben—it was immediately apparent, even to strangers, that we were lovers, from the aura we cast over each other when we were together. Ben was the type of man as comfortable in shorts as in a suit, outside in the park as indoors reading a book. He had a controlled, suave temperament but a wonderful imagination. I remember how, after seeing a movie, he could create a whole new plot from a single line of dialogue. But I think what I loved most about Ben was his ability to look at the future—our future together. He was always suggesting places for us to go, things for us to share. Ben had been burned and spurned in all of his previous relationships. And when we met he was as eager to be in love as I.

o

I had a feeling I would see Scott again. It was a week after Ben's death and I had gotten up early, found Batello's leash, and snapped it onto his collar. Together we set out in the direction of Castro Street. When I had met Scott in the doctor's waiting room, I thought I had noticed him once before near the corner of Market and Castro. Ben and I would often walk in that direction, stopping at one of the shops before heading back to our apartment. I remembered I had admired a young blond man through the glare of an afternoon sun, standing beside a folding table, asking pedestrians to sign a petition. That morning I hoped I would find the young man again and that he would be Scott. But I also had another feeling, a much more startling sensation. I felt it was time to let go, time to move on, and from the simple action of walking, or even Batello dragging me along the streets, it would happen. I knew it was time to forget that Ben had died.

When we reached the intersection, Scott was not there. There was no table. Batello was straining to sniff a hydrant, so we continued walking. I noticed, as we approached 18th Street, that there was a table sitting in a patch of sunlight, and as we drew closer I saw Scott distributing pamphlets to passersby.

I veered Batello in the direction of the table. Scott did not look at us when we approached, but I took a pamphlet as we passed by the table. We had moved toward the table in a crowd of other men, and Scott had tried quickly to place a piece of paper in each of our hands. The other men continued walking. I stopped by the table and stared vacantly at the paper. Batello sat on the sidewalk and looked up at me.

"How's the allergy?" Scott recognized me, approached, and patted Batello on the head.

"Dead," I answered, knowing it made no sense in response to his question. I could not look at Scott; instead I stared at the words of the pamphlet, warnings of medications thought to be hazardous if used in treatments.

My hands began shaking. I realized I still did not have the strength for a sustained conversation, but I knew exactly where my thoughts were headed. I was trying to let go, trying to connect with Scott, trying in some sort of frantic way to stop from going crazy.

"Which way you headed?" Scott asked, and put his pile of papers on the table.

"Nowhere in particular," I answered.

"Why don't you meet me at the gym on Market Street in a half hour?" he said.

A sigh raced across my body, a jarring gasp for breath that crested and disappeared like a wave breaking against the shore. This must be what it is like to let go, I remember thinking. I dropped the sheet of paper, and Batello watched it float to the sidewalk. I never thought I would reach a point in my life where I felt like I was drowning—floundering and fumbling without any sense of direction.

Scott must have noticed it. The sinking.

"You got to keep moving," he said, and took Batello's leash from my hand. We began walking. "There are days I don't feel like doing anything. But I know, even when I force myself to do something, I feel better afterward. You've got to find something that makes you feel better, and do it."

I knew then that I needed help, and with the realization came again that lightness, that pleasant, dizzy feeling inside my head. I still needed to let go. But by then I knew exactly what I had to do. I had to change my way of thinking.

o

"You're too romantic," Mark said one night when I was at his apartment. "So was Ben." It was two weeks after Ben had died. Mark was cooking again at the stove. He turned off the burners and sat across from me at the table. "Me, I went straight for it. I can remember all the places I used to look for sex. But I can't remember the men. I remember the action of the sex more than I remember who it was with. It's funny sometimes what stays in your memory."

Maggie the cat scampered underneath the table and began to weave between my legs, rubbing her sides against my jeans. "But

I do remember romance," Mark said, and leaned down to pet Maggie, who had worked her way over to his side. "About nine years ago, I noticed a guy following me on the street. At first I thought he was somebody I might have slept with before, someone who wanted to do it again. But he didn't approach me. And he kept following me for several days. Then I got a letter, then another and another. Then the letters started coming every day. They weren't sexual letters. They said things like, 'Your beauty is brighter than a thousand stars,' and, 'I could never imagine someone more attractive than you.' I don't know how I knew it was him, but I did. He found out where I worked. He sent me flowers and presents. But he never did anything to meet me.

"It got to be kind of bizarre. He was always at the same bar, or out dancing where I was. But he never approached. Never said anything to me. I used to point him out to friends. But I remember after a while I got used to it. I got to depend on it, in a way, especially after some of the dreck I dragged home. One night I was walking home in the rain and there he was on the corner. I asked him if he wanted to come up for a drink. He wasn't that unattractive. He actually looked sort of nice. I certainly wouldn't have thrown him out of my bed, because I had bedded worse. So, what the heck, I was caught up in the romance of the moment. The idol pursuing the admirer.

"When he was here, I asked him what he wanted. He said he wasn't sure. So I pounced. We had sex. I remember the sex was great. We did it in a thunderstorm, a damn thunderstorm that lasted for hours. And then I never saw him again. The letters and presents stopped. I wonder if that's what he wanted. The sex. Or if the sex dissolved the illusion of romance, or that maybe he realized that neither of them, sex or romance, is a guaranteed path to love."

That evening, at home, I lay awake in bed. I could not sleep. Men kept dancing, spinning, and twirling through my mind. Tall men, husky men, blond men, rugged men, bronzed men, businessmen, athletic men. Men of all ages and shapes, heights and wits. I kept trying to make them disappear, but they kept dancing, whirling between colored spots of light shooting down from the recesses of a black, smoky ceiling. I could not figure out why these men would not disappear. So I kept watching them dance until I found the answer.

I had invited them into my memory.

One night ten years ago, I drove four hours from my Alabama town to Atlanta to discover these dancing men. I went to investigate my feelings, to understand who I was trying to be. I needed to see if what I felt was unique or if there were others who shared my proclivities. And I had heard there were dancing men in Atlanta. And there, in a crowded disco with blinking lights and thunderous, rowdy music, I became enchanted. There I knew it was all right to want to dance, to want a man. These were men who felt as I did. And I decided to join in the dance. The image of coming out into a world of dancing men has forever shaped my consciousness. And with this image, this belief, this decision to belong in this world, I received many invitations.

My first invitation to sex came from a man who had first asked me to dance. Another man carried me away from Alabama, and we danced together for almost six months in North Carolina. And it was there that the dancing and the sex became integrated, gave me an identity, and thrust in front of me adventures I could never have imagined. It was another dancing man who transported me to New York, the same man who disappeared shortly thereafter at the invitation of another dancing man. But I did not mind; I now had an identity. I had sex. And it was this sex that dressed me and led me through the streets. It was sex that sent me invitations to parties and bedrooms. It was sex that introduced me to the men who became my friends, the same sex that sent me searching through the parks, streets, stores, and bars. It was sex that kept me dancing.

And so I lay there that night in bed alone, wrapped and protected by my belief in dancing men, yet aware that my knowledge of this dancing, this sex, had subconsciously defined my expectations. I wanted to imagine what it would have been like with Mark or Scott as a lover. What it might be like. What it would be like. But my belief and knowledge kept the speculation rooted in reality, and I understood what Mark had meant when he said that sex was not a guaranteed path to love. And the expectations, the desires, the dreams of what I wanted had become a sequence of evaporating hopes.

And I remembered, too, that night, why I had left New York. I had lived in the city for seven years and been through a succession of jobs—first as a messenger for a law firm, then as a bartender in a nightclub, and later as a typist at a hospital, a salesman in a department store, and, finally, a researcher for a marketing firm. I was not driven to find a career; that was not the reason I had moved to the city. And when I left New York, I had every intention of returning. My roommate, Jack, had suggested I take a vacation. Jack, a short, paunchy man in his fifties who had made a career out of arranging Caribbean cruises and Mediterranean tours, said I was burned out. He said I needed to relax, clear my head, fly away from all the perimeters. The dancing had stopped, or at least I had stopped dancing. I had stopped because I was taking the world that dancing had generated too seriously. It had created an obsession to be surrounded by desirable men. It demanded a ritual of what to wear, what attitude to assume, and when to assume it. It provoked the excess to maintain the good time—the magic, the beauty, the high—through whatever drugs or drinks I wanted to try. And the result was the expectation that participating in this frantic revelry would guarantee an even better time in bed, which in turn, I had hoped, would lead to something more permanent, a relationship that not only involved sex but was also grounded in commitment, caring, companionship, and trust. I stopped dancing when I recognized I was being driven by desire. I was waiting for something to happen, something or someone to keep me dancing.

Jack had sensed my growing depression and recommended I travel a bit, perhaps even go somewhere distant and exotic for a while, such as China or the Far East; I had saved some money and he knew I could afford the trip.

"You should stay away from anything tropical," Jack said to me one night. "You don't want to be anyplace where natives walk around undressed."

I mentioned I wanted to go to Europe; I had never been abroad before and had always felt a poetic yearning to see what it was like. But I wanted to find a place that felt both familiar and foreign, a place that would interest and absorb me.

He frowned and answered, "Not London, dear. It's becoming too much like New York."

He went to his desk and found a map, returned to the couch, and spread it across his lap. "Paris is out, because you want to wait to go there with someone special. Amsterdam is pretty but the nightlife is too wild. Bavaria can really be boring if you're not into castles and mountains. Vienna is a little too grand for your tastes, I think. You'd be disappointed in Greece, but Rome and Milan are quite wonderful."

"What about Venice?" I asked, looking where his hand had fallen on the map.

"Venice," he whispered. "Now there's a place you could get lost."

o

I often wonder why it is the rain that makes me remember how it felt. Perhaps it is the grayness of the sky, the way the wind can alter the direction of a falling shower, or the sense that the world is cleansing itself. Or perhaps it is the chill which sometimes accompanies it, penetrating the skin, stinging the joints of fingers and toes. Whatever, rain, and sometimes even the touch or nearness of water, can make the feeling come back to me, as perceptible as the cut from a razor.

When I arrived in Venice, it was in a torrential rain. The hotel room in the Dorosduro, where I was staying, was even smaller and more cramped than the bedroom of my New York apartment. And the rain did not stop. After the second day of wandering aimlessly through the streets, I felt as if my umbrella were surgically attached to my hand. I had stopped in a café behind the Piazza San Marco when another downpour had made even the aimless roaming impossible. There was a group of tourists behind me who were insistent on sitting outside, underneath an awning, but I went inside and took a seat at an empty table in a corner of the café. At the moment when even the pigeons were fleeing to the ledges of the buildings to escape the rain, the tourists finally abandoned their tables to settle inside. Everyone began laughing. Chairs were rearranged so that tables could be shared. And the man who came to share mine was Ben. He apologized for his intrusion and the way he must look; indeed, I remember he was quite a mess. His hair was dripping wet; his white shirt and tan slacks were streaked with gray from where he had scraped against the stones of dirty buildings to avoid the rain. It was Ben who later said that if I could fall in love in a moment like that, then it was a love he had no doubt would last. But I had laughed and said it was not like that at all. It was the moment of a stranger in a strange city sitting with a stranger, connected simply by the fate of the weather.

Even wet and disarrayed, Ben had the dark, sleek looks of an Italian, though I could tell when I had first noticed him that he was not a native by the curiosity of his eyes. He explained he was an economics professor from San Francisco and had been attending a conference in Geneva when he decided, impulsively, he wanted to visit Venice. We spent the next four days together, in the afternoons, dodging the rain to see the Galleriè dell'Accademia, the Palazzo Ducale, and the Basilica dei Frari. In the evenings we stayed at Ben's hotel room; I had abandoned mine, though Ben's was not much larger: a bright yet musty accommodation with a lopsided floor and peeling strips of plaster the size of flags on the ceiling, furnished with a white canopy bed and fading tapestries on the wall. There were drinks at Harry's Bar, a shopping excursion to the markets of the Rialto, and a morning visit by boat to the island of San Michele, all journeyed beneath umbrellas. On the last day, on a rainy trip at sunset beneath the Bridge of Sighs, Ben asked if I would consider living with him in San Francisco.

I told Ben that life in San Francisco would not be the same as a vacation in Venice. But I was not surprised when the plane landed in New York and I could not leave the airport. Ben had given me both romance and sex. Now he was offering more. I have never considered myself an impulsive person, but that day I bought another ticket and continued on to San Francisco. Sometimes, when something that is not devised or deliberate strikes, it can simply carry you away.

○

There were twenty-two other men in the room besides myself and Scott. Twenty-two men I had never seen before. There was one woman, a middle-aged blonde: a short, thin woman who seemed dwarfed by the men in her presence and who kept lifting her eyebrows to make the tiny black dots of her eyes appear larger.

"I am not here to impart information," she explained when everyone was seated, "but to help you share your feelings."

"This is not an act of desperation," Scott had said before we took our seats.

"We must visualize the end of this virus," the blond woman continued. "We must see it as a newspaper headline or a television broadcast, a news report announcing its termination. We must try to see it dissolving and disappearing into the vacuum of the universe."

The twenty-two strange men in the room closed their eyes. Scott closed his eyes.

"Nothing lasts forever," the woman said as I closed my eyes.

There was not another word spoken in the room. In the silence I tried to imagine what this woman had asked for, but instead I could see only myself, standing at the end of a pier, the wind blowing lightly around me. It was a memory from two weeks before, three days after Ben's funeral. It was early morning, and when I had left the apartment I ran for many blocks, traveling by instinct across the hills and streets to the pier. And when I reached the end of the pier I ignored the world behind me; the park, the stores, the people, were not there. It was only myself and a box I had carried from the apartment. I opened it and ripped the plastic bag inside apart, pouring ashes into the water, trying not to think about what I was doing. I did not feel I was fulfilling a wish that had been left behind in a note, a hope of washing away any trace of guilt. It was merely something that had to be done. And when it was completed, I left the pier.

But when I returned to the street, I felt as if I had been thrown into a bottomless pool, my arms and legs listless, immobilized from the weight of the water. I had to remember that in order to stay afloat you have to stay in motion, you have to kick your legs and flutter your arms. In order to walk you have to move one foot in front of the other, swinging your arms from side to side. And in order to find my way home I had to remember which streets to take, where the sidewalks and signs would lead me. I knew exactly how these things should be done and where I should be headed, but I could not link the mental knowledge with the physical action, making something as simple as crossing the street require an intense, complicated concentration.

"I am not a doctor," the blond woman with the tiny eyes had said, breaking the silence. "I cannot cure anyone. But I do try to help people change their lives. I try to teach people that, if they restructure their beliefs, they can remold their existence. They can better their lives. To do this, you must focus on the positive."

I tried to remember my feeling that day when I had finally found my way back to the apartment. I had sat on the couch, shocked and grateful that I had made it safely home. But I felt a depression looming over me, making me shrink into the couch like a speck of dust. I couldn't shake the image of myself on the pier, emptying ashes into the bay.

"I have never considered killing myself," Scott said to the group of men and one woman. "I wouldn't even know how to do it. Something inside me tells me I must try to live as long as I can, that in doing so, in trying all the treatments, something might work—something so that someone else will not have to go through what I have. It's the only thing I have left to offer, so I have to offer it with all my heart."

Five days after that day on the pier I returned to work, returned to the tiny little desk on the second floor of an accounting office in a building on Embarcadero. I did not need to explain where I had been or what had happened. My co-workers knew Ben, knew all the details about his death. But I was still too new for many of these people to offer me condolences. I had worked there only two months.

And so, that first day back, I worked in silence, adding, subtracting, and balancing the figures on ledger sheets, while everyone sidestepped my discomfort with downcast eyes and trembling hands. It was Gary, Ben's friend who had found me this job, who tried to pry open the grip, the grasp between one who lives and grieves and one who is dead.

"I've been praying for you," Gary said to me when we were alone, near a storage cabinet that held office supplies. Gary was tall and slim, with a body that appeared to be all bones and angles. He had an intense blue-eyed gaze and a nervous habit of running his fingers through his wild black hair before slanting his body to speak to someone shorter. "Gary and Richard had been lovers, off and on, for twelve years," Ben had explained one night when we were eating at Mark's. "When Richard died, Gary flipped out. He was in a psychiatric ward for a while, and someone brought him a Bible. When he got out, he carried that Bible everywhere."

"It was real annoying at first," Mark added. "But he never tried to provoke an argument or anything. We realized it gave him something to talk about. We called all his friends and told them to tolerate it. We told them *why* they had to tolerate it. He didn't lose a single friend because of God."

"God works in mysterious ways," Gary whispered, leaning toward me and pushing away the hair which had fallen in front of his eyes.

I remember I did not answer him. I could not even look at him. I wanted to tell him to save his breath for other sinners. I had met God only last week. God was a stocky forty-year-old man with a receding hairline and a gray-flecked mustache who had walked into my apartment and washed the dishes and changed the sheets. But I did not tell him. I wanted to tell him that God had even spoken to me, but I did not. "Get up," God commanded me. "Shave," He ordered me. "Shower," He pushed me. "Drink this," He said, and set a cup of coffee before me. God was not offering me any consolation or sympathy or understanding, only immediate actions. "Get out. Go for a walk," He prescribed before He left. "Do something. If you have trouble, call this number." After God left I called the number but got a busy signal. God was preoccupied, talking with someone else.

I walked away from Gary and returned to my desk. He followed and stood over me when I sat in the chair. He continued to speak as though he had never been in love with another man.

"You must never forget that the ultimate relationship is between God and yourself," he said. "Not what you had with Ben. Know that and you will know God."

"Please." I finally spoke to him, not looking, just speaking. "Don't," I said firmly, in a tone I meant to make the conversation stop.

"God is with you always," Gary said.

I wanted to tell him what I thought about God. I wanted to tell him that if God was always with me, then it was God's fault Ben was dead. If God was present with me the day I sat waiting to see the doctor about an allergy, it explains His absence from

Ben. He should not have been with me. He should have been with Ben. I said nothing to Gary about God's flaw, and began racing my finger over the buttons of the adding machine.

Later that day, Gary returned to my desk and left me a note. "Believe in God and He will provide you with the answers," it said.

No, I thought. God cannot answer my questions. He cannot tell me where Ben has gone, yet He can shatter my achievement that day when I finally calmed myself, got up off the couch, and went into the kitchen for a glass of water. And when I sat down again I noticed, on the bottom of my legs, large smudges of the ashes I had just cast into the bay. He cannot tell me where Ben's soul is resting, but He can smear his death into my skin. He cannot tell me if I will ever see Ben again, but He can make the memory of Ben's life haunt me. I only wanted a life as orderly as the ledger sheets before me. I wanted a formula that provided a clear solution.

"I have no answers," I said to the woman, looking away from Scott and the twenty-two strange men. "The questions are always changing."

o

No matter how successfully I was able to let go during the day, to move on, to forget, my desperation for Ben would return at night. Some evenings I was able to fight it off by drinking or taking pills. Most nights, however, my loneliness would prevent me from ever falling asleep. I would lie in bed in the dark, staring at the ceiling or watching the light which drifted in through the window from the street traffic. Some nights I would simply lie and watch Batello watching me. Batello had begun to sleep on the floor the day after Ben's death. Sometimes I would reach down and scratch his head, and his eyes would lift up to mine, and I knew he was just as confused as I was. Sometimes I would pat the bed and he would leap up and sleep beside me. But there were nights he refused to budge, his head between his paws, staring at me, waiting for me to tell him when Ben would come home. On those nights I would pile pillows on the bed, trying to re-create the body which once lay beside me, trying to find another way to fall asleep. But most nights I just stared at Batello, or stared at the ceiling, or stared at the shadows swimming across the wall.

I don't remember exactly when I started walking around the apartment in the dark. I think it was the night I thought that if I turned on the radio, the sound, the noise, would create enough distraction so that my mind would allow me to fall asleep. I remember holding my arms up that night, into the light from the window, noticing the darkness of the hair on my skin, the way the light folded around my wrists and then bent into the darkness of my palms. It was then, that night, I think, that Ben first came back to me as vividly as when he was alive. I could smell his skin, his shaving cream, his underarms. I could taste his breath, his morning stubble. I could feel the fine curls of his hair, wet after showering, and the cleft of his chin. I could feel him lifting my body into a great hug, as he often would, trying to spin me around as though I were a rag doll.

And then I remember, every night afterward, I began to get out of bed and stand in the darkness of the center of the room, waiting for Ben to hug me and lift me into the air. Sometimes I remember him cupping my chin and tilting my head back as he always did, but before kissing me he would dance me around the room. Night after night he would dance and dance with me. Every other man, every other spinning, twirling, whirling man, disappeared to me except for Ben. I could feel my body once again covered by his fingerprints, his breath against my neck, my heart jumping and alive. Some nights, while we danced, I would notice

Batello looking at us, his eyes wide and surprised. I kept Ben dancing as long as I could, as long as I needed him beside me in the darkness.

And I remember the mornings I would awake and find myself curled on the floor beside Batello, his dark, sad eyes once again staring into mine.

○

It was a Saturday night, three weeks after Ben's death, when I met Scott for dinner at a café on Jefferson Street. The weather was warm and we sat outside on a terrace, underneath an awning, with a candle on our table, eating, talking, and watching the couples stroll by. After dinner, we ourselves set out on a stroll, peering at the novelties that lined both the streets and the stores of Fisherman's Wharf. We continued walking for a while, until we sat on a bench in the park above Ghirardelli Square. The sky was clear that night, and the stars above twinkled as brilliantly as the lights of the bridge and the city. "When I first moved here, I used to walk here all the time," Scott said. "There were so many lights. It was so different from where I came from. Ohio was flat. You could only see one light at a time."

When I first moved to San Francisco, Ben and I once stopped at this same bench. It was a rainy afternoon, and before we sat, Ben dried the bench with a towel he carried in his gym bag. We sat underneath an umbrella, and Ben pointed out a building where he hoped we might one day live, because, as he said, the view was spectacular. I told him I was happy where I was, and we began to talk of how we wanted to spend our summer. Ben wanted to learn how to sail and knew of a lake in Canada where he had heard beginners could try their luck. I wanted to tell Scott all of this, that I had agreed with Ben about the sailing, but I did not. I wanted to tell him that I, too, had wanted to learn to sail. I wanted to tell Scott that I had laughed and only agreed on one condition, that this time, wherever we went, we would invite the sun to accompany us. I wanted to tell Scott that Ben had smiled and closed the umbrella and we had sat in the rain, but I did not. I had decided our evening of stars and lights should remain our own.

Later that night, we walked to Scott's apartment, and on the street beneath his window, Scott asked if I would like to come up for a drink. "Club soda," he said, laughing, when we reached the top of the stairs. "It's all I have."

Inside, after we had finished our drinks, Scott sat on the couch and I positioned myself in a chair. "I can't tell you how I feel, because I don't know," Scott began slowly, carefully. "I can't tell you what the pain is like, because I've never been through this type of pain before."

He stood and walked to a table near the door, found a letter, and carried it back to the couch, where he sat and read aloud. " 'Dear Scott,' " he began. " 'I am a mother of three children. My oldest son, Craig, is a carpenter and lives with his wife in San Diego. My daughter, Linda, is a travel agent and is married and living in Portland, and is expecting her first child, and my first grandchild, in September. My youngest son, Patrick, was a computer technician and lived in San Francisco until he died last month. When we were cleaning out his apartment I found his address book, and your name and address inside. I am writing this letter to let you know that Patrick has died, in case you didn't know already. Patrick fought against cryptococcal meningitis for nine months, but died after his second hospitalization from pneumocystis. I am not writing to sadden or scare you, I only want you to know I am proud of all my children and that I have loved them every day of their lives. Sincerely, Mrs. Baker.' "

Scott placed the letter on the couch. "I don't even remember him."

That night I stayed at Scott's apartment. We lay in bed together, and when I felt his body slide into sleep, I avoided closing my eyes. I was not afraid of sleep or dreams. I was not afraid of the dancing men. And I knew I would not need to resurrect Ben to dance with me that night. I was wide awake, ready to go on living. Scott awoke and noticed I was not asleep. "I wish it was different," he said and closed his eyes and fell back asleep. It was then I knew my life was changing again. I had decided to make Scott my responsibility.

o

"I know he means well, but, God, he is so tedious sometimes," Mark yelled one afternoon and flipped a Bible in my direction. Ben had been dead for six weeks.

We were at Mark's apartment, surrounded by cartons of cardboard boxes. I placed the Bible on the coffee table and then held the flaps of a box down as Mark taped up the edges.

"You'll remember to water the plants," Mark said. "The lady downstairs will come in once a week to clean and dust. Gary will check the mail. I'll call you to let you know if you should send the boxes."

Mark carried the box to a closet, where he placed it on top of several others. I walked to the window, opened it, and leaned my head out into the warm air. Maggie the cat jumped on the window ledge and sat beside my arm. On the street below I watched Scott help Gary put a suitcase in the trunk of Mark's car.

"He's really nice," Mark said. "Take care of him."

On the street Scott leaned against the car, smiled, and folded his arms. Gary brushed his hair from his eyes and leaned over to speak to Scott.

"I thought I could handle it," Mark had said when I joined him for dinner a week before that day of packing. "I thought I knew how to handle it. The therapy is fine for that one hour, but I'm finding I need more. There are just too many distractions here. I keep remembering the way things used to be. What I used to do. I was walking on Castro Street this morning and there was this guy with the most incredible chest I've ever seen. He was absolutely stunning. With a tan, no less. It's bad enough to have to live with this plague, but to have to look at something like that prancing down the street . . ."

It did not take Mark long to decide to leave San Francisco, though he said that it was only temporary, for the summer, and that he would be back when he got his head together. Mark had only recently found out he tested positive; the lesion he had discovered on his thigh had been diagnosed as Kaposi's sarcoma. He was moving to a cottage his sister owned in the mountains of Colorado, a cottage he explained was only an hour away from his parents' home. "There's not a gay man within miles," Mark had said, laughing, when he told me his plans. "At least none that anyone suspects. It's odd how the family takes you back in the end," he said. I knew he was right. I knew, if I was in Mark's situation, that I, too, would probably return home to the Alabama town I thought I had escaped.

"I never told you Ben called me from Venice," Mark said that day, when we had finished with the boxes and he was wiping the counter with a sponge. I had followed him inside the kitchen and was stacking clean plates in the cupboards. "He called and said, 'I've met my desert flower.' He was referring to you." Mark smiled at me. "Ben and I used to rent a Mercedes convertible and drive to Palm Springs for the fun of it. There were so many beautiful boys just standing on the streets. It was always an amazing experience for him. Beauty in the midst of all that hot, dry desert. He called those boys 'desert flowers.' I knew Ben a long time. I know he was never happier than when he died. I think that's why he went so quickly. He wanted to go while he was happy."

The inside of my chest felt crammed, distended. I held my breath, trying to make the feeling disappear.

"You'll get over him," Mark said, and threw the sponge into the garbage. "It just takes time."

I did not answer. As we walked through the apartment I knew it was not the boxed-up memories or the closing and locking of the windows which saddened me; it was the offer of time from someone who might be running out of it.

I lifted the last suitcase from the floor and followed Mark toward the door. He stopped by the mirror in the hall and looked at his reflection. "We were never meant to grow old anyway, were we? Look at these goddamn bags under my eyes."

As I watched him disappear from his reflection and scoop Maggie the cat into his arms, I remember wondering if I would ever see him again.

o

It's hard for me to reconstruct the months that followed. Time moved erratically; some days would pass swiftly, others lingered, vacuous and unremitting. At first Scott's illness was only a series of minor irritations, a cough which would not disappear, bouts with diarrhea, and a general malaise which could be rejuvenated by naps. We saw each other frequently, meeting for dinner after work, alternating spending nights at my apartment or his. Then I discovered, quite by accident when I phoned his office one afternoon, that he had started to leave work early, and not much later learned he had begun to miss full days. When I asked him about this he explained he could no longer control his exhaustion, possibly a side effect, he said, of the combination of new medications the doctor had prescribed. His voice had become low and hoarse, which he thought was from a lack of sleep, and I noticed he had started to lose weight. Sometimes he would be sullen or grumpy, other times his temper could flare over something insignificant: a hole in a sock or a misplaced book. For a while he tried to push me away, avoiding my phone calls when I knew he was home, and finally, one night, refusing to open the door of his apartment to let me inside.

"I can't," he said through a crack in the doorway.

"Why?" I asked, annoyed, my arms full of groceries that night.

"It's not fair," he answered.

"You can't blame yourself," I began, knowing where this conversation was going, having started and stopped it with him many times before. "It's not your . . ."

"No, to you," he interrupted.

"I'm not complaining."

"I'm just going to pull you down with me. I can't do that to you."

"You must not know me very well," I said, "to think you can get rid of me just because you're not feeling all right."

"You never knew me when I was really happy," he said, and started to cough.

"But I know you now and I want to come in."

I knew his depression was mounting, but I also recognized his stubborn will, his refusal to admit he was beginning to need help. But I could be as stubborn as Scott, and a few minutes later he had reluctantly let me inside.

In bed that evening he tossed fitfully, unable to sleep. Holding him, though he was sweating, I could feel his body shivering. Holding him tighter, I could sense a new brittleness in his bones;

his skin felt as thin and delicate as paper. I remember that night was the first time I really felt helpless. I wanted Ben to appear, lift me into the night, and dance me away from all of this.

"Move in with me," I said to Scott, finding an uncertain strength, my voice reverberating against the darkness of the bedroom.

"What?" he asked.

"If you're worried, move in with me."

"No," he answered. "It's not going to get any easier."

It was not easy to convince Scott to move in with me. But I made him, realistically, confront his options. He could stay in his apartment and rely on the help and support of his friends, worrying about paying his bills if he could no longer work; or he could return to Ohio and live with his parents. But his parents, as I reminded him, were not even aware he was ill. And what about the availability and control over his medications and treatments; would he be able to manage those in Ohio? I reminded him of his other options: he could move in with another friend—several had offered—or he could eventually end up in a treatment center, though I knew this was not an alternative he wanted to consider. There was a part of me that felt selfish in forcing him into a decision, but I honestly felt it needed to be resolved, and I knew, perhaps most of all, I wanted to be with him as much as possible. At that point I realized I needed Scott as much as I knew he needed me.

It was Dale, Scott's best friend, who finally convinced him to move. Dale, a corporate lawyer, had known Scott since college. A solid, athletically built young man with prematurely graying hair at his temples and a solemn attitude of assurance, Dale, for years, had helped Scott with his finances. Recently, he had closed Scott's checking account and sold his small portfolio of investments, holding Scott's money in his own personal account, from which he paid Scott's bills. When he came over one night to Scott's apartment and I mentioned my suggestion, Dale turned indignant and told Scott, "Do you think you're going to walk into a bar and find a better offer?" Later, I learned they had once been lovers, though I never discovered why their relationship had ended and they had decided to remain friends; I can only imagine it was because they were simply both too headstrong for one another. There were times when I was jealous of Scott's trust in Dale. Often Scott would call Dale for advice, knowing he would get a fast, rational answer. But there was a night when Dale stayed after Scott had gone to sleep, and while we sat watching television he said to me in his brisk, efficient tone, "You mean a lot to him." And then, before leaving, added, "I'm scared, too. I have every reason to be."

I tried my best to make Scott comfortable at my apartment. Scott said he was willing to leave everything behind, though I knew him better than that. Dale and Gary and I packed his books and records, and rearranged my furniture to make room for Scott's couch and bookcases and the antique Victrola he had inherited from his grandmother. Ben's clothes, which I could never before touch, let alone relinquish, I gave to friends or donated to charities. I sent Ben's books and papers to the university library. Most of his personal belongings I threw away; some items—his souvenirs from Europe, his college diploma, and a painted ceramic dish where he used to keep his car keys—I mailed to his father in Arizona. His wallet, watch, and photographs I packed in a box to save for myself.

When Scott moved in, his spirits fluctuated even more wildly than before. There were days when he would refuse to shower or leave the apartment; sometimes he would begin crying when he looked at himself in the mirror, noticing how his skin had become pasty and white and his hair had thinned and started to recede.

In the mornings he would sit in bed and watch me get dressed. I knew he was comparing our bodies; I could see the frustration etched in his stare. At times his anger could be extremely bitter or violent; worrying about the success of a new treatment, the loss of sensation in his left arm and leg, or his inability to concentrate or read, he would throw whatever was within his reach against a wall, tear up a pillow or a T-shirt, or start yelling till he lost his voice. I knew he was beginning to feel defeated, though there were moments when he would be ecstatic, recounting for me the plot of his favorite soap opera or a game he had played with Batello. His health began to improve when he stopped taking the steroids the doctor had recommended to maintain his weight. And there were even days when nothing appeared to be wrong, though often, at night, lying in bed, his head on my chest, he would press his hand against mine and say, "Tell me a story. Take me away from all this."

There are fragments of the time I spent with Scott that are so distinct they seem as if they happened yesterday: the way he would lie on the couch watching television with Batello curled at his feet; the way, when sleeping, he breathed through his mouth; the way that, the day we drove through Napa Valley to find a new restaurant, he insisted, with a laugh, that we drive down Lombard Street on the way home, late at night. Many things I have simply forgotten; others I have blocked from my memory.

Dale and Gary were frequent visitors, accompanying Scott on trips to the post office or the bookstore, or to get a haircut. Often one or both would join us for dinner. One night Gary handed me a postcard he had gotten from Mark. I knew Mark had moved in with his parents, and the card, from Denver, had been sent by Mark's sister. It read, optimistically, "Doing better. Will be back for a visit soon." The month before, Gary and I had moved everything out of Mark's apartment, and when we knocked on the superintendent's doors, I noticed, for the first time, as Gary handed over the keys, a sorrow overtake his posture. There was so much information I wanted from Gary. What was it like, what had happened when Richard was sick? Some evenings, when Scott had gone to bed, I would describe to Gary, over the phone, meticulously, the events that had happened that day. I always waited for Gary to say, "With Richard, he . . . ," but the advice, the details I wanted to know, were never forthcoming.

"God does help, you know. He does care," Gary would instead say.

"Yes," I would answer. I had asked God several times for help.

God appeared to me many times in those months. He was a high-school boy who delivered lunches to Scott, a young woman who offered to do laundry, a neighbor who would drop by in the afternoons to see if Scott wanted to play cards. I saw God in the actions of friends, escorting Scott to doctors, picking up his prescriptions, bringing him a new magazine or video to watch. I felt God through the touch of a nurse, smelled Him when Dale brought Chinese take-out, heard Him when Mark called one night on the phone and asked to speak with Scott. But I could never understand that the God who was showing such compassion and kindness was the same God who had disrupted, almost to the point of destruction, a basic conception of my life, my love for another man.

o

I have not been able to forget Ben a single day since his death. I have been reminded of him by articles in the newspapers, by reports on the six o'clock news, by his friends and mine calling to ask me how I am, by the details I have to attend to as the executor of the small estate he left behind, details which can be mundane, annoying, or time-consuming, such as sorting through bills, writing letters, or photocopying his death certificate. And on the sidewalks, walking, where I think my actions, my movement, will pull me away from his life and back to my own, I see reminders of him in the people who pass: one man has his eyes, another his profile, others his eyeglasses or his out-turned walk.

When I visited Scott in the hospital I thought I had come to terms with all of it. I thought I had a grasp of the situation. I thought I was getting stronger. Scott was sitting in bed looking through a magazine when I entered the room.

"This floor has the most gorgeous interns," he said in the raspy whisper his voice had become as he looked up at me. "There's this one Italian. . . ."

He stopped. He must have read my eyes.

"I've spent the day making lists." The tone of his voice changed and he showed me a pad of paper on the stand beside the bed. "I can tell you at least forty-seven things that make me happy besides sex. I can name eight people besides my family who I have truly loved. I can tell you fifteen therapies I have tried to stay alive. I can think of seventeen ways I would rather die."

I did not say anything. I placed the pad of paper on the bed and walked to the window.

"You did this because of him, didn't you? That's why you helped. That's why you're here, aren't you?" Scott asked.

I did not need to answer.

"I know why he did it," he said. "It's in your eyes. He didn't want to see it. He was afraid of watching you watching him die. That's why you came to me. You needed to watch someone die, in your own mind, to justify his death."

Outside, I noticed it had started to rain. I left the window and sat on the edge of Scott's bed and took his hand in mine. His fingers were chilly; his arm, where it had been prodded with needles and intravenous tubes, was a patchwork of purple veins and bruises. He had not shaved in two days and his neck looked as raw and thin as a twig of a winter tree.

"I'm not bitter," he said, and ripped up his lists. "I'm thankful I have someone here. I only hope that what you feel will not pass away with death."

The feeling did not pass away with death. Scott was released from the hospital in two days, but two weeks later he was back. Another bout with pneumonia. He died a month after that first visit to the hospital, eight months after Ben had died. The last week, I was there every day. I never left his side. I was there when the fluid which filled his lungs made him drown.

The last week Scott was in the hospital, I told him the story. I didn't have to, he told me. I didn't have to go through it again, he said. I wanted to, I replied to him. I wanted him to know. I told him that when I came home from the doctor's office that day I first met him, I had met the old woman, Mrs. Tenna, who lived upstairs from our apartment. She was slowly climbing the stairs with two bags of groceries in her arms. I offered to carry the groceries up to her apartment, and when we reached the third floor, where she lived, she invited me in for a cup of coffee. She told me she had lived in San Francisco for thirty years and had been born in Denmark. She had married a man who had sailed her off to Boston, and when her husband died, she married another, who took her and her two children west. First to Seattle, where her husband worked for an airline, and then for a while to Texas. Her third husband had moved her to San Francisco, a city she said she loved and decided to stay in after his death, because her children had married and lived nearby, in San Mateo and Oakland. She had been everywhere, she told me, from Wheatland, Wyoming, to Egypt, only to end up here now, an old woman struggling to climb to the third floor with two bags of groceries. No regrets, she said, and smiled when she finished her story. And I remember feeling relieved that she had distracted me from the fear the doctor had caused. And when I went back downstairs to our apartment, Ben was asleep in the bed, Batello lying beside him atop the bedspread. I wanted to wake Ben and tell him the doctor had said my rash was due to an allergy, just as he had expected, but I didn't. I let him sleep. I went into the living room, turned the stereo on softly, sat on the couch, and read the newspaper until Batello sprang into the room and began to lick my hand. And then I began to have difficulty breathing. I got up from the couch and went into the bedroom. Ben wasn't sleeping. He was dead.

I told Scott of the horror of the rest of the day: the visits from the police and detectives, the arrangements for the funeral, the phone calls to Ben's family and friends, the arrival of the mortician, and the way they carried Ben out of the apartment on a stretcher, zipped in a dark, airless plastic bag. I told Scott I knew why Ben had done it, but I was afraid of believing that was the reason. Ben had not wanted to drag me through months, maybe years, of his being ill. He had left me a note that said he loved me too much to put me through that. I didn't want to admit that that was the reason, but I did that day. And I told Scott that was why I had found out where he was. Why I had made a point of finding Scott, meeting him again. I didn't want him to die alone. I had to go through it. I wanted and needed to understand.

o

I used to think the world was divided into us and them, that I was part of a secret society, a fraternity of men, as it were, who could distinguish one another by discreet clues and codes: a style and fit of clothing, an expression of body language, the lingering contact of eyes. Yet I always knew I was not immune to the rest of the world; after all, I was a product of their environment. I was raised by parents with a standard of morals, a belief in honesty, freedom, and trust, who instilled in their children equal portions of politeness and guilt. But by the age of thirteen I knew I was different from my parents, detached by some other schism than the separation of generations. I remember one night lying on the floor of our den watching television, becoming disturbed as I watched a man kiss a woman; I knew my curiosity was part sexual arousal, yet I was confused about why I was more attracted to the man, imagining what it would be like if he were embracing and kissing me. I began studying men carefully, the way the sweat formed on my father as he mowed the yard bare-chested, the way the older boys at school touched themselves as they showered in the locker room. I started locking myself in my bedroom, staring at the pictures of athletes in magazines, memorizing the firmness and energy of their bodies, fantasizing they were next to me, touching me, wanting me, needing me. I read every book I could find on sex, even the ones my parents kept hidden in the back of their closet, alarmed and even more confused by the descriptions of homosexuality as a deviation and a perversion. My senior year in high school, I began traveling at night to Atlanta, the next day explaining my absence to my exasperated parents by saying I had been at a game or out with friends. And I thought that, as I grew older, life would begin to make more sense, that the education and rebellious confusion of my teens, the explorations and efforts in my twenties, would emerge and settle into some sort of cognizable conclusion. Now, having just turned thirty-three, I realize that the more I learn, the less I know. My father, at this age, had a career as an engineer, a wife, three kids, two cars, a house, and monthly mortgage payments. Sometimes I think all I have now that is tangible is my anger, my embitterment, my disconsolation because of death.

Death, until now, has been an infrequent visitor in my life. My parents, grandparents, and brother and sister are all healthy and alive. I had an uncle who died in a factory accident when I was eight, but he lived far away and his death was only mentioned one morning at breakfast; no sorrow, no change, were perceptible in my parents' behavior. Often I think it is not so much death that now maddens me, but the extinction of those I know who are too young to die: death, as it were, from an uncontrollable war.

I can't say what grief is harder: the loss of a parent, a child, a sibling, a spouse, a lover, or a friend. The night I called Ben's father, the day I met Scott's parents at the hospital, the morning the phone rang and a tiny, tearful voice announced that she was Mark's sister and that he was dead, I felt I had no monopoly on grief. But were they aware my sorrow had more depth than anger? Did they understand my fear: that this could just as easily have happened to me, could, in fact, still happen?

There were many years when I disregarded my parents, presuming geographical distance would keep us out of each other's thoughts, believing any discussion of my life would make them embarrassed, ashamed, or unable to accept and understand. Parents, of course, do not want their children to be different from themselves. After Scott's funeral I called my parents, and when my mother answered the phone I began to explain to her some of the missing sequences of my life. I wasn't trying to scare her or make her upset; I wasn't seeking her blessing. All I wanted was some facts to be known: what had happened, the way I lived. My mother said she would tell my father, who was not at home, of our conversation. And then she asked if I wanted her to visit. "Not yet," I answered, and felt, for the first time in many years, that misery, that spasm of sudden unhappiness, which is homesickness, of a child wanting his parent to protect him from the outside world.

When Scott died I thought I would feel that something had come to an end. But now, almost a year since Ben's suicide, I am still amazed at how stirred up I am, a man stirred up about sex and death. I thought at the end I would move away from San Francisco, but I have not. Instead, Batello and I have moved to an apartment near the harbor piers.

But I have gotten a new job. Now I work in a store near Fisherman's Wharf, a store which sells T-shirts and souvenirs to people who pass by on the street. And my allergies have long since disappeared, thanks to the medication a new doctor prescribed, and the man who owns the store where I work lets Batello sit by my side.

I thought, perhaps, if I started over with a new home and a new job, I would forget about what had passed. I would forget about Ben and Scott and Mark and Richard; even Gary and Dale would slip from my memory. But, like the life I had had before them, the Alabama youth, the invitations to dance, the sexual quest of New York, they were now, irrevocably, a part of me. With no regrets.

o

There is something wonderful about the way a man dances, the way the hips move back and forth or in and out, the shoulders shift to heavy rhythms of music, the feet twist in a way not possible when walking. There is something wonderful about watching a man dance, the eyes darting to follow an attractive figure weaving between patterns of light and sound. There is something wonderful about dancing with a man: eyes, shoulders, hips, and feet balanced, connecting to a synchronous beat. There is something wonderful about dancing, enrapt in the magic of music and motion.

A month ago I decided to go dancing; I had this crazy urge to know if there were still men dancing. I showered and dressed and went to a disco I had once heard Ben mention. The men were still there. But this time I did not wait to see if there were any invitations; I did not wait to find out if these men were dancing the way I used to dance. Instead, I stepped out on the dance floor by myself and unlocked my most important secret. Action does help smooth the pain. The muscles began vibrating beneath my skin, and a feeling of motion began pushing me forward. Dancing, I could release the frustration, I could ease the heartbreak of death. I could forget for a moment about this plague. I could forget about sex. Dancing suddenly became a physical pleasure, not a philosophical quest. And I was aware that for the first time in my life, I was not afraid of dancing alone.

Now, every evening when I leave the shop, Batello and I walk to the park near the piers before we return to the apartment. I throw a stick and he retrieves it. I did not teach Batello this trick. That is something Scott had done, and Batello, I believe, finds it as much a joy to carry the stick in his mouth and drop it in my hand as I do to see how far I can throw it. Three weeks ago, when we were walking on the pier, I stopped and asked a man who was scrubbing the deck of a sailboat if he could teach me how to sail. He gave me one of those looks, the kind that go up and down the body, smiled a little nervously, and said he would. His name is Neal and he is quite handsome: tall, dark-brown hair, deep-blue eyes shaded by silver wire-rimmed glasses, and about five years older than me. Besides teaching me how to sail, Neal has asked me out on two dates; the first time we went out for dinner, the second to see a movie. But the happiest moments I have with Neal are when Batello and I sit on the deck of the sailboat. With one of my hands holding on to a rail and the other holding on to Batello, I watch the wind flap the sail, Neal tug a rope and steer the rudder. Batello and I lift our heads into the wind, feeling the breeze rush up from the water and sweep across our faces. The day after Ben's suicide, Mrs. Tenna knocked on my door. She had heard about Ben. She knew all about the way he had willingly swallowed a fatal combination of pills. She walked into my apartment and threw a bucket of water on the bedroom floor. We both stood and watched it puddle. Ghosts cannot cross water, she told me. She said it was an old custom. Her mother had done it before her. There is a moment, just before the sun sets, when Batello and I are on the deck of the boat, the wind blowing our hair in every direction, when I want to find a stick and throw it as far as I can, as far as my arm will toss it, hoping it may cross the water and fall safely on another land. But I do not. I believe in ghosts. I really do. I have to believe in something. For now.